"A pity perhaps that I cannot be kind."

An ironic smile curved Azir's strong, sensual mouth. "But that wouldn't work for me, would it?"

Ashley couldn't follow his meaning. "It never hurts to be kind."

"Then will you be so . . . to me?" The soft appeal was so unexpected that it confused Ashley. She struggled to understand what this abrupt change of manner meant. "Stay here as my guest," he added.

"And if I don't want to stay?" she pleaded.

He stroked her cheek in a softly mocking salute. "I'm afraid I cannot give you any choice in the matter. Until the course has been run."

He still meant to have her!

And she had nothing to fight him with anymore. Slowly she lifted bleak eyes to her nemesis. "Then I'm not your guest. I am your prisoner."

Emma Darcy nearly became an actress until her fiancé declared he preferred to attend the theater *with* her. She became a wife and mother. Later she took up oil painting—unsuccessfully, she remarks. Then, she tried architecture, designing the family home in New South Wales. Next came romance writing—"the hardest and most challenging of all the activities," she confesses.

Books by Emma Darcy

HARLEQUIN ROMANCE
2900—BLIND DATE

HARLEQUIN PRESENTS
935—THE IMPOSSIBLE WOMAN
960—WOMAN OF HONOUR
984—DON'T ASK ME NOW
999—THE UNPREDICTABLE MAN
1020—THE WRONG MIRROR
1033—THE ONE THAT GOT AWAY
1048—STRIKE AT THE HEART
1080—THE POSITIVE APPROACH
1103—MISTRESS OF PILLATORO

Whirlpool of Passion

Emma Darcy

Harlequin Books

TORONTO • NEW YORK • LONDON
AMSTERDAM • PARIS • SYDNEY • HAMBURG
STOCKHOLM • ATHENS • TOKYO • MILAN

Original hardcover edition published in 1987
by Mills & Boon Limited

ISBN 0-373-02941-1

Harlequin Romance first edition November 1988

CHAPTER ONE

SHE would do it, Ashley decided. So what if it was a stupid, irresponsible idea! No one would ever know about it. No one that mattered. She was half a world away from home, and answerable to no one as far as her own personal financial position was concerned. If she lost the money, it wouldn't drastically affect her life, but if she won . . . to help Sohaila into a happy marriage would give her more satisfaction than anything had given her in years.

Common sense told her she was clutching at straws. The odds against her winning the amount Sohaila and Ahmed needed were undoubtedly astronomical, but Ashley was fed up with being sensible. At least trying something positive was better than remembering the misery on her friend's face.

Ashley knew that kind of misery all too well, the deadening sense of futility that came with fighting something that couldn't be beaten. She would never forget the despair of those last months of her marriage, trying to face up to what couldn't be faced, suffering Damien's pain with him, knowing she could do nothing to help except be there. And in the end her being there had eaten away his will to live. She had been no help at all.

Ashley dragged her mind off those torturing memories and glanced at her watch. She had seen the advertisement in the hotel elevator often enough to know that the casino opened at nine p.m. It was now almost eleven, late enough for the gambling tables to be in full operation.

This was a once-in-a-lifetime experience, Ashley thought grimly, as she searched through her clothes for something suitable to wear. She had never been inside a casino, and the rather unsavoury glamour attached to such a place was a little unnerving. Not to mention the fact that she was totally ignorant of games of chance. What she needed was something classy but inconspicuous, and her choice fell on the long-sleeved black dress she had bought at Harrods in London.

Despite its modest style, it was the most deceptively sexy dress Ashley had ever worn, and she hesitated a moment before pulling it on. She had had a few discomforting experiences in Egypt, fending off the unwanted attention of the local men. But there was nothing to fear in this hotel. The Cairo Sheraton was a perfectly safe harbour for foreigners. It was not as if she was wandering abroad. The casino was only six floors below her own.

Ashley loved the rich sheen of the black silk brocade. She had loved the elegant lines of the dress from the moment she had first tried it on. The sleeves were slightly puffed at the shoulder line to add featured interest to a bodice that was starkly sculptured to the generous swell of her breasts and clung to her body long enough to emphasise her narrow waist and the feminine curve of hip before slicing to a V-line across her stomach. The skirt was artfully pleated on to the V, accentuating the hip line, then narrowing to just below the knee.

Sheer black stockings and black patent leather high heels were the perfect complements, and Ashley piled her long tawny-blonde hair into a gleaming loose chignon on top of her crown to set off her fashionable attire. She touched up her green eyes with a subtle make-up, added a blush of colour to her cheeks, and carefully applied her favourite coral-red lipstick. Then, ready to face any critical eye, she slid the cheques she needed into her evening bag and took the elevator to the second floor.

Casino—the discreet gold lettering at the side of the doorway brought a twist of uncertainty to Ashley's stomach; but the lure of quick money, big money, the kind of money Sohaila needed, drew her feet to take the decisive step inside.

The moment she entered the plushly carpeted lobby Ashley feared she had badly miscalculated her timing. There was no noise; no hum of conversation nor clink of glasses to suggest a crowd of carefree gamblers. The darkly panelled walls enclosed an almost funereal hush, which was emphasised by the subdued lighting.

The impulse to turn tail and forget the whole idea was stilled by the interest of the two men behind the reception desk. Some perverse pride insisted that she go on, and she adopted an air of studied nonchalance. She could pretend she was looking for someone and walk out again in a few minutes if the situation didn't suit her. There was no need for panic.

'Your nationality, *madame*?'

The question startled her. Was there some special procedure necessary before being allowed into a casino? She looked blankly at her inquisitor until her nervous gaze caught the sign—'No Egyptians may go past this point'.

'Australian,' she replied with a smile of relief.

The man smiled back at her. 'May I wish *madame* good luck?'

'Thank you,' she breathed, then walked quickly on, feeling the speculative gleam in the dark eyes behind her.

Her spine crawled uneasily. Sohaila had told her that the morals of any unescorted Western woman were suspect in Egypt. Apparently there were women who came here precisely for the purpose of having a sexual fling. Their reputation tarred everyone else. Ashley considered this dreadfully unfair, but there was nothing that could be done about it.

When Sohaila had explained the situation, Ashley had been shocked, and yet she could understand the attraction of Egyptian men. They were spectacularly handsome, with their beautiful dark eyes and brilliant smiles. Under different circumstances she might have appreciated the admiration that had caused her discomfort, but Ashley could never think of sex without remembering Damien.

She shuddered and concentrated her mind on her present purpose—to help Sohaila towards the happiness that she herself had been denied.

A tingle of excitement warmed her as she paused at the top of the steps which led down to the gaming-room. It was not as large as Ashley had expected, containing only three roulette tables and two others where card games were being played. All the tables had drawn their measure of players even though they were not yet crowded.

No one took any notice of her and she instantly understood the lack of noise. All concentration was focused on the fall of a card or the spin of the roulette wheel. Gambling was obviously a lonely, intense occupation, not even superficially social.

The croupiers made their calls in low voices. The click of playing chips being placed or removed was the dominant language being spoken. Ashley noted with wondering curiosity that the faces around the tables were completely impassive, showing no joy at winning or disappointment at losing. It seemed incredible that the money meant nothing. Was it bad form to show emotion?

An abrupt movement at the roulette table directly below her caught Ashley's attention. A bulky man in a fawn suit spun the seat of his stool around and heaved himself off it, leaving an inviting vacancy. Ashley did not want to take up a playing position yet, but the space did give her a clear view of what was happening. She moved down the steps and stood behind the stool. The croupier gave her an encouraging nod, but she shook her head and kept her distance.

'Would *madame* like a drink?'

One of the silent-footed waiters was at her elbow. 'Yes. A gin and tonic please,' she decided quickly, feeling in need of some extra fortitude in this strange atmosphere. The drink was swiftly brought and Ashley opened her bag to pay the man.

'No charge, *madame*,' he informed her quietly, and as she glanced up, startled, he discreetly added, 'All drinks in the casino are free.'

'Oh! Thank you,' she rushed out, grateful that her lack of *savoir-faire* had been so tactfully corrected.

She nursed her drink, feeling rather guilty about accepting it when she wasn't playing. But she intended to, she promised herself, as soon as she knew what to do.

A betting card gave Ashley all the information she wanted. A maximum of a hundred dollars on a straight-number bet returned three thousand five hundred, but the odds against any one number coming up were too prohibitive, and she would need three wins on those to collect the amount Sohaila and her fiancé needed. On the black market, ten thousand American dollars could be changed for eighteen to twenty thousand Egyptian pounds. With that extra amount the pair could buy the apartment they wanted and start their marriage without the dreaded in-laws breathing down Sohaila's neck and dictating how her life should be lived.

However, Ashley did not have the heart of a gambler. Her more cautious eye was drawn to the even-money bets; black or red; odd or even; 1-18 or 19-36. She could place a thousand dollars on those and all she had to do was win ten more times than she lost.

Of course, no bet was safe. Common sense reminded her of that. Ashley watched the play for over an hour, recording the result of each spin of the wheel on her card. She found that black or red often came in a three or four sequence before changing. Sometimes it went longer. However, the very essence of gambling was its unpredictability, so she couldn't rely on these patterns continuing for any length of time. If she was going to hazard the thousand dollars, it was better to do it now before she lost her nerve.

Her heart accelerated with nervous excitement as she walked purposefully towards the money-changing counter to convert her traveller's cheques into the American dollars necessary to buy the chips. The face of the man behind the grille held a bored expression. Ashley wondered just how many thousands of dollars passed over this counter each night.

Her hand shook a little as she picked up the hundred-dollar bills and crammed them into her black, beaded evening bag. She took a deep breath to quell the slight flutter in her stomach, then turned back towards the tables.

The flowing white robes of the Arab caught her eye. Pristine white. Clearly of the finest linen. Most of the Egyptians wore the long dress-like *galebaya* with a turban or skull-cap on their heads, not the more graceful head-dress that this man wore.

But then he couldn't be Egyptian. Not here. Perhaps he was a Saudi, or from the UAE, or Kuwait or Bahrain. Whatever he was, he held a posture of command and authority which was impressive.

He stood at the top of the steps where Ashley herself had paused. Something that Sohaila had told her clicked into her mind. The thick twisted *'iqal* that fastened the Arab's head-dress was made of golden cord. Ashley had never expected to see it worn, and certainly not at close quarters. Only people of royal blood were allowed to wear it.

Ashley stared at him in fascination. He was not exactly handsome, nor even particularly attractive. The eyes were too deeply set in their sockets, the nose too hawkish, the mouth too full-lipped, but somehow the sharp cut of his cheekbones and the hard thrust of his jaw stamped him with an impression of power that was aggressively masculine. He literally emanated the kind of charisma that would always force attention.

He surveyed the room below with a slow, careless arrogance, almost as if he was considering if it was worth the waste of his time to enter. With an abruptness that caught Ashley by surprise, the dark gaze stabbed straight at her, fastening on her with such a searing intensity that it made her skin burn with self-awareness.

An uncontrollable surge of defiance fired her own gaze straight back at him. It was a sexual challenge that was totally instinctive, without thought or reason, fracturing the numbness that had characterised her reaction to men since Damien's death.

Danger prickled down her spine, but for some unaccountable reason, Ashley found the sensation delicious. She felt herself vividly alive in a way she hadn't felt for over three years. Perhaps it was her decision to gamble a thousand dollars away tonight that made her feel reckless. Or perhaps it was a rebellion against the Arabic assumption that Western women were immoral. In any event, she'd be damned if she would lower her eyes in modest rebuttal of the blatant desire in his. Let him think what he liked; it wouldn't do him any good.

What made her do it, she didn't know. Nor did she stop to question the mad impulse. She walked towards the gaming table with a roll of her hips, deliberately flaunting her body in front of him. Some fiercely awakened devil relished the gleam of lust it brought to those dark, flashing eyes that raked her from head to foot.

A satisfied little smile tilted his lips, giving his mouth an extraordinary sensuality. And a twist of cruelty. Ashley's heart pumped an alarm which she sternly repressed. It was exciting her too much, the way he looked at her. She could not tear her eyes away from his. It was exhilarating to make this arrogant Arab look at her like this.

A thrill of power danced through her veins and she exulted in playing with fire, uncaring of what might happen next. She had never expected to feel the thrall of sexual awareness ever again, but it was pulsing through her now with a force that insisted upon being savoured to the full.

He did not move. He watched her all the way with unswerving intensity, and Ashley was more physically conscious of herself than she had ever been in her life; conscious of the silk of her stockings brushing between her thighs; conscious of the rounded thrust of her breasts pressing into the fabric of her dress; of her delicately pointed chin tilted high above her long, golden-tan throat; of the tendrils of tawny hair dangling down her smooth cheeks; of the weight of the long, thick, sun-streaked tresses piled high on her crown; and she knew that her clear green eyes were no longer their usual cool. They were flirting with the ignition of volatile passions.

She had never been a tease, and never wanted to be. It was crazy, what she was doing, flagrantly inviting trouble, but she could not stop herself. Not even a quivering sense of disloyalty to Damien acted as a deterrent. Somehow this man was drawing a reaction from her that set every nerve in her body vibrating with exultant, primitive life, and not once in her twenty-eight years had she felt anything like it.

She judged the most tantalising moment of imminent confrontation, then swung her back on him, and in an elegant movement, slid her bottom on to the still vacant stool at the roulette table. She could feel the dark eyes burning along the row of covered buttons that ran down the curve of her spine, and she had a mad, hysterical urge to laugh. She felt free, free in a way she had not felt since Damien's illness had destroyed their relationship and driven him to take his own life.

The croupier smiled at her and Ashley returned a dazzling smile that quite startled him. He raised his eyebrow questioningly, but she shook her head, too dizzy with wild sensation to concentrate on betting right now.

The wheel was turned. The man on her right lost the last of his chips and left his stool. He had been sitting just around the corner of the table from her. As he moved, Ashley heard a faint rustle of cloth behind her and her heart leapt into her throat. She knew who it would be. Even before she caught a glimpse of his white robes from the corner of her eye, she knew it had to be the Arab.

Her whole body tingled with an electric awareness as he took the place vacated. She wanted to look at his face, wanted to see if the desire was still in his eyes; but she no longer dared. He was too close, too dangerously close if she was to keep some control of the situation. She had been unbelievably mad to challenge such a man. How she was going to defuse the situation was still beyond her, but sanity insisted that she give him no more encouragement.

A wad of hundred-dollar notes was carelessly thrown upon the table. The croupier checked and rechecked them, then slid them down the money-slot. Ashley counted the twenty-five-dollar chips pushed towards him. There were forty. A thousand dollars.

The darkly tanned hands curled around the chips. Strong hands, with long, supple fingers. They placed half the chips on black, the other half on odd.

Ashley sat absolutely still, her gaze inexorably fixed on those very deliberate bets. Black and odd. Was that because of her dress and her behaviour? She had no doubt that it was a statement of some kind, designed to gain her attention.

Well, he wasn't going to win it that easily, Ashley determined. She relaxed as the sense of power rippled through her once again. He could do whatever he liked—she did not have to respond to anything he did. Yet caution whispered that a man who bet a thousand dollars on a mere whim could not be taken lightly.

She removed the betting card and pen from her evening bag, and was pleased to see that her hands were still steady. The tourneur set the roulette wheel in motion. Other players kept placing their chips until the croupier called, 'No more bets, please.' A few moments later the ivory ball clattered into its final resting-place.

'Fifteen.'

Black and odd. Ashley made a note of it on her card. The brown hands reached out and took the winnings, letting the original bets stand. A gold signet ring on his left index finger winked teasingly at her, but she did not look at him.

In what seemed like a gesture of careless contempt for any system of betting whatsoever, he tossed the chips on to the numbered pattern of squares on the table, and showed no interest at all in where they fell. The croupier shifted some that had scattered outside the betting area, raising his eyebrows at the Arab as he moved them to the closest square. He received no audible reply.

Obviously money meant nothing to him, Ashley thought with a touch of envy. And resentment. These blood-royal Arabs could throw it around like so much confetti. For people like Sohaila and Ahmed it meant the difference between a marriage that was independent of their families and one that would be torn with dissent.

The wheel was spun.

'Thirty-three.'

Black and odd won again. The Arab had the luck of the devil. Some of the chips had fallen on thirty-three, others on the line-bets around the number. Stacks and stacks of chips were pushed down to him. Again he left the original stakes on black and odd. All the others he had won he placed in front of Ashley. His hand gestured an invitation.

'Play with these, *mademoiselle*. Perhaps they will

give you the courage . . . to commence betting.'

His voice was low and pleasant, but the challenge implicit in his words goaded Ashley into a reply. Mentally harnessing all the nerve she possessed, she slowly tilted her face, and lifted her gaze to his. His face was close enough for her to see the lines of ruthless purpose stamped on it, and the eyes . . . they were the eyes of a man who could kill if it were necessary, or take forceful possession of anything he wanted.

And he wanted her. He did not give a damn about the wedding ring on her finger; could not know she was a widow. The man was amoral, a devil who meant to take what she had so recklessly offered, and he meant to take it tonight. There was no mistaking his intent. Nor the undiluted lust burning in those dark, brilliant eyes.

It raised no fear in Ashley, but rather injected a burst of adrenalin through her veins that heightened a compelling sense of contest. She could feel the tentacles of his will reaching out to dominate her and the excitement of locking her own will in battle with his was more than she could resist.

She smiled and returned the French address that was more common in Egypt than any English form. 'Thank you, *m'sieur*, but I don't need those chips any more than you do. I pay my own way.'

Ashley did not wait to see his reaction. She opened her evening bag and tossed her thousand dollars on the table, copying the nonchalance he himself had displayed. His low laugh played havoc with her pulse, but she steeled herself against any crack in her calm composure. He could not win with her unless she let him.

The croupier took her money and served her with the same number of twenty-five-dollar chips he had given the Arab. Ashley ignored them, disdaining to place a bet until she was ready. The wheel was spun. The Arab did not make any other bets, apparently content with those still placed on black and odd.

'Twelve.'

Red and even. He had lost. Ashley barely repressed a grin of triumph as the croupier scraped her adversary's chips back to the roulette bank. The run of blacks had ended. She waited for the Arab's next move. Without any hesitation at all, he placed a five-hundred dollar stack of chips on both black and odd. He was going to lose again. She felt as sure of that as it was possible to feel sure of any gamble. He would lose and she would win. It had to come up red again. By the law of averages ... but there was no law of averages in gambling, she reminded herself.

Nevertheless, logic was a weak voice at this heady moment. She craved action. Successful action that would show this man that she was no weak-hearted woman. With every appearance of complete sang-froid she placed the thousand dollars worth of chips on red, but her heart raced faster than the wheel as it spun the ball towards its ultimate destination. It seemed to go on for an eternity before the ball lurched from the rim into a pocket. Ashley waited for the call; she could not bring herself to try and look at the wheel.

'Seventeen.'

Black and odd. She stared disbelievingly as the croupier placed the winning marker on the number. Black ... and odd. She had lost, lost the lot. A thousand dollars. She had told herself she could afford to lose it, but she hadn't really expected to. Not all of it, not on the first spin. It had been utter madness to do what she had done. Madness! All motivated by stupid pride ... and the challenging presence of the Arab.

She hadn't even thought of Sohaila and the money that was still needed to buy the apartment. The Arab had taken over her mind. It was all his fault. If he hadn't ... No, she couldn't lay the blame at his door. She had chosen to play against him. She had gambled and she had lost.

'A brave plunge, *mademoiselle*,' came the soft, insidious voice, the challenge in it subtly muted to a note of provocative approval. 'All or nothing. I like that.'

Ashley still felt shaken by the suddenness of the loss, but she turned towards him, opening her hands in ironic self-deprecation. 'Reckless folly! It's the end of the game, *m'sieur*.'

'No. I can't allow it.' He smiled and it was the most dangerous smile Ashley had ever seen. Even the white gleam of his teeth seemed to radiate a confidence that undermined her own. 'You haven't got what you came for,' he added with a flat certainty that Ashley immediately wanted to shake.

'Then I must leave without it,' she tossed at him carelessly.

'What were you trying to win?'

Ashley raised mocking eyes to meet his. 'Only ten thousand dollars. Nothing else, *m'sieur.*'

'How totally foolish!'

The scorn in his voice made Ashley blush. No point in trying to explain a shattered dream, or a quixotic desire to help someone else to a better life. No point in telling him it was all done in the name of love. His cold ruthlessness would never understand such sentiments.

She rested one hand on the table as she levered herself off the stool. Strong, warm fingers covered her own, dark on golden-tan. It was a fascinating juxtaposition and for one wild moment Ashley wondered what it would be like to have his whole body covering her own, what it would be like to be possessed by a man who exuded so much raw power. His fingers curled around hers, sensing her moment of weakness and playing on it.

'I must go,' she said thickly, having to force herself to fight the physical magnetism he was exerting.

'Not until you have what your heart desires, *mademoiselle.* That takes total commitment. I'll show you how to do it.'

'No...I...' Her voice was swallowed up by the mad temptation to give in and be shown whatever this man could show her.

'Think of a number, any number on the table,' he commanded softly.

'Don't be absurd,' she whispered, but there was no conviction in the way she said it.

'Tell me your number.' His voice was hypnotic.

'You can't do it!'

He merely smiled. The need to challenge him swept her again.

'Twenty-three.'

'So be it.' His eyes were predatory and chilling. He picked up a bundle of chips and looked hard at the tourneur, as if he could direct the turn of the wheel by the sheer power of his will.

'You can only bet a maximum of a hundred dollars on a number,' Ashley stated defiantly. 'Even if twenty-three comes up, you will only win three and a half thousand dollars.'

'If twenty-three wins, it will be red. I place a thousand dollars on red. Another thousand on odd. Five hundred dollars on the column, five hundred on the range of numbers from twelve to twenty-four, and another thousand on the numbers nineteen to thirty-six.'

Her mind whirled through the figures as he calmly placed the bets. He was laying out over four thousand dollars. If the number did come up the return would be eight and a half thousand dollars, plus the stakes. Nearly thirteen thousand dollars in all!

The wheel was set spinning; the ivory ball revolved around its perimeter. Ashley could not drag her eyes away from the Arab. It was madness; he couldn't win. It was a crazy, flamboyant gesture, doomed to failure.

The croupier cried, 'No more bets, please.'

The brown hand tightened its grip on hers as the ball tumbled towards its final destination. A faint smile touched the croupier's mouth.

'Twenty-three.'

Ashley stared disbelievingly as the winning marker was placed on the number. Piles and piles of chips were pushed down the table to rest directly in front of her. Her mouth went dry.

'It's yours,' the Arab murmured in his low, seductive voice. 'To do with as you wish.'

Ashley snapped out of her mesmerised daze. She had read of oil-rich Arabs handing over fantastic gifts to people who had won their favour for some reason or other, but Ashley believed that such gifts had to generate a sense of obligation upon the person who received them. There was at least a subtle pressure for goodwill in any future dealings.

If she took what he was offering her now, it would almost certainly imply an acceptance of him and all that he was. And Ashley wasn't prepared to do that ... was she? Nothing could be more certain than that he only wanted one kind of relationship with her, and that was purely physical.

Her eyes lifted and met his with fiery pride. 'You misunderstood me, *m'sieur*. The money means nothing to me. I merely wanted to help out a friend.'

He shrugged. 'Take it. Your pleasure is mine.'

'No. Your pleasure is not mine, *m'sieur*.'

He raised a sardonic eyebrow. 'You play with words, *mademoiselle*, but your actions are far more eloquent.'

Ashley couldn't deny it. Even now her body was reacting to him; the touch of his hand, the wicked promise of his eyes. But she couldn't just walk off with him and share his bed, no matter how deeply tempted she was. It was totally irresponsible, dangerous and stupid.

Self-respect warred with the desire he had planted in her and somehow emerged the shaky victor. She lifted her chin in pointed disdain and forced a proud scorn into her voice. 'And you, *m'sieur*, are gambling again, and this time on impossible odds. You have lost, and the game is over.'

'I do not gamble, *mademoiselle*. And I always win.'

A gleam of hard ruthlessness brought a sharper intensity to his eyes, and Ashley felt pinned by them. She nodded towards the table, needing to rock his arrogant assurance. 'If you don't gamble, *m'sieur*, what do you call those bets you placed just now?'

A slight twitch of his lips drew her attention to their suggestive sensuality. 'Perhaps I wanted to play at being . . . your God. Perhaps you struck a chord of compassion in me. What does it matter? I want you to have the money you came for. Take it. It's yours.'

She could not accept that there were no strings attached to it. No one gave away sums of money like that on a mere whim! And the way he was looking at her ... devouring her. Not even for Sohaila could she take that money. It would mean a surrender to his will, and Ashley was frightened to think where that might lead.

'You misunderstood me,' she repeated vehemently and snatched her hand from his.

He was too potent, too mesmerising. If she stayed with him any longer she might be persuaded into some further madness she would surely regret. The only sane thing to do was escape as quickly as she could. Without uttering another word, Ashley swung on her heel and marched off up the steps.

CHAPTER TWO

ASHLEY made her escape from the casino and was a few metres down the corridor when she heard him behind her.

'Come back!'

The soft call made her step falter. She turned, seduced from her intention by the sheer magnetism of the Arab's presence. His hand was stretched out to her, inviting her return.

'You are no coward!' he continued even more seductively. 'Why do you run away before we have barely brushed the surface?'

Impossible even to pretend misunderstanding. Ashley needed all her will-power to resist the tug of his powerful attraction. 'We inhabit different worlds, you and I,' she cried in a desperate attempt to drive a wedge of cold reality between them.

'The meeting-place is here and now.'

The meeting-place for what? A mingling of their flesh? It could never be of minds. His way of life, views on social issues, customs ... all so different. Alien to everything that had formed her life. 'No, it's not possible,' she insisted, and forced herself to turn away from him and keep walking.

He followed her, his pace unhurried but undeterred by her rejection. The soft thud of his footsteps pounded in Ashley's ears, but she did not turn round. She strode along the corridor towards the elevators, doing her best to hide her inner agitation. She walked stiffly, trying hard to negate the sexual promise she had suggested before, but her body was pulsing to the possibilites that had simmered between them.

As great as the temptation was to explore those possibilities, Ashley could not contemplate doing so. She was here in Egypt on a mission of enormous responsibility, negotiating with high-level officials in government. She had won their respect and she wasn't about to lose it by plunging into an affair with an Arab who was probably well known to them.

It appalled her that she could even want to do such a thing. She had never indulged in casual sex, not before her marriage and certainly not since. The idea of a purely physical relationship without any emotional ties whatsoever, without anything in common but a mutual need . . . it ran counter to everything she believed in. There had to be something more. It was wrong, this desire she felt. It had to be terribly wrong.

Almost in a panic at the attraction the Arab was still exerting, Ashley jabbed her finger on the up-button for an elevator, then whirled around to face him, forcing a frosty dignity she was far from feeling.

'Please go back. Your chips will be stolen if you leave them lying on the table unattended.'

The dark gaze probed the fearful confusion in

her eyes. 'No one will touch them. They are safer there than in any Western bank.'

'I don't want you with me,' she blurted out, denying the feverish pumping of her heart.

He stepped towards her. Ashley shrank back, hard against the wall, frantically willing the elevator doors to open and provide her with a ready escape. He lifted an arm, placing his palm flat on the wall near her ear.

'I'll scream if you touch me,' she whispered shakily, her breath constricted in a throat so tight that she could barely swallow.

His face came closer, his eyes commanding hers with relentless purpose. 'You want to taste me as much as I want to taste you.'

There was time for her to turn her head aside. His mouth approached hers with a slow deliberation that taunted the throb of need inside her. She could not stop her lips from quivering in anticipation. It was recklessly wanton of her to concede. He was dangerous. But somehow the arguments her mind conjured up didn't sound as good as tasting what this man was offering.

All the frustrations of the day curdled the last bastion of common sense. She had wanted a decision out of the Egyptian officials on the jewellery of the Pharaohs. She had wanted to help Sohaila. Nothing had worked out right. And now she wanted . . . craved to know whether this strong desire she felt was a wild fantasy, or fact.

His hand moved from the wall and curled around her throat, caressing the intense tension that held her motionless. His thumb tilted her chin. His mouth took possession of hers, ruthlessly pressing the desire that tore through her belly and drained the strength from her legs.

His kiss was merciless, smashing through every inhibition with an aggressive eroticism that had all of Ashley's senses reeling into chaos. All thought of resistance was driven from her mind, lost in a whirl of sensation that peaked into passion when he swept her body hard against his. Her whole being vibrated in wild response to his. She was utterly helpless to stop him from doing anything he wanted with her.

Ashley didn't want the kiss to end. It was as if she had been starving, and she could not bear the feast of sensation to be taken away. A little animal cry of need dragged from her throat when his mouth withdrew, and he rubbed his cheek against hers as if in loving comfort for her distress. His harsh breathing fanned her ear with a tingling heat that grew more intense when his warm lips brushed close to her lobe and whispered his triumph.

'You cannot deny what we have.'

The softly spoken words dropped into the whirlpool of her mind and formed chill ripples of sanity that lapped at the edges of her senses, forcing an acknowledgement of reality. No matter that this man was filling needs and desires that had lain dormant for years; it was still madness to succumb.

She did not even know his name. And what

manner of man was he that he should kiss her like this, here where anyone might come along and see them? The lateness of the hour was the only reason why they had not yet been interrupted.

With slow, seductive sensuality his mouth trailed kisses around her temples, down her cheek, and her head turned instinctively to the command of his lips. The shreds of her will-power were hopelessly weak. How they drew the necessary strength, Ashley never knew. Even as she tore herself out of his embrace, the shock of loss left her shaking.

He caught her easily. His hands flashed out and encircled her wrists, pinning them effortlessly between her breasts as he dragged her back to him. Alien, her mind screamed, as her frightened eyes flashed a confused appeal to the dark, hawkish face that stared so demandingly at her.

'Why do you fear the pleasure I can give you?'

Was it pleasure? Her whole body was a tremulous mass of shrieking nerve-ends. What he could do to her was no fantasy, but she couldn't let it go on or she would lose all control. 'I don't fear it,' she insisted, but the words were furred with a tumult of conflicting emotions.

He laughed softly. The black ruthlessness in the depths of his eyes still had the power to shake her to the innermost parts of her body and mind. She knew she had to escape him if her life was not to be inexorably changed. What had already happened sent a flush of shame to her pale cheeks.

But even as her mind feverishly reasoned

against him Ashley could feel what little strength she had mustered draining away. Her gaze flicked despairingly to the elevators. They were notoriously slow in responding to a call. And if one did come right now, would this man even hesitate to accompany her up to her room? How could she stop him?

'I wish to go free, *m'sieur*,' she said, doing her best to inject a calm, reasonable tone into her voice. 'If you don't release me now, I shall yell for help.'

One black eyebrow rose in amused disdain of her words. In sheer panic, Ashley tried to drag her hands out of his hold. The sharp movement caught him by surprise and his grip slipped to her fingers before closing hard to prevent her escape.

'Please . . .' Ashley whispered, hoping to reach some spark of humanity in him.

His eyes looked into hers, dismissing the plea and probing straight to the need that pulsated within. 'You cannot go free, any more than I can. The bond is already forged and you cannot escape it.'

Ashley tried to laugh at his arrogance, but no sound came forth. Her stomach was tied in knots, twisting to the tug of his presence. Self-survival depended on her getting away from him. She swallowed hard, desperate to work some moisture into her arid throat.

'You are wrong, *m'sieur*. I've had all I want from you and I don't need you for anything more,' she said harshly, driven by his forcefulness to be cuttingly blunt. He had stirred her out of sexual apathy, but she simply couldn't allow any further intimacy between them.

He smiled that slow, dangerous smile, his eyes glinting with a mockery that was edged with supreme confidence. 'Your need matches mine and I see no peace from it.'

He lifted her hands and pressed a kiss into each palm and, although his grip on her had gentled and she could easily have snatched her hands away, Ashley simply stared at him in helpless thrall, her arms weak and utterly useless as the warmth of his kisses tingled down her veins.

'Shall I prove it to you again?'

Once more he gathered her close. The experience of his previous kiss ravaged Ashley's will to resist, and when his mouth took hers she surrendered to his will with a wanton abandonment that cared for nothing but his possession. She had lost all sense of self by the time the elevator doors slid open beside them.

'Come with me now. We will learn all there is to know about each other.'

His arm was pulling her towards the compartment when a thread of sanity finally struggled through the web of dependence he had woven with his kiss. Horror billowed through Ashley's mind. In blind panic she tore herself out of his grasp and ran for the great marble staircase that led to every floor of the hotel.

'Stop!'

The sharp command stabbed at her heart, but

Ashley did not stop. She knew what he could do to her and it terrified her. Her legs felt like jelly as she pushed them up the steps. Her whole body seemed to be shaking out of control. She paused to catch her breath on the next landing and flung a frightened look down at him.

He had started after her. He was directly below her on the opposite side of the stairwell. Even that distance did nothing to mitigate the searing power of the dark gaze that pinned her there, clutching the brass banister in a convulsive need to feel some barrier between them.

'No! No!' she cried, her voice shrilling in hysterical need to deny what she had so very nearly done. Then, driven by the spectre of such madness, she clattered on up the stairs, wishing she could take her high heels off and hitch up her narrow skirt. But he was watching her and she didn't dare stop again.

She had bolted up three floors and there were still three more to be negotiated when the realisation suddenly struck her that all he had to do was stand in the stairwell and watch her and he would see what floor her room was on. The staircase spiralled around itself so it was possible to see right up to the roof. She felt certain that whatever means he employed to find out her room number, he would do it. She had to think how to avoid that happening.

Trying the lifts was no good. They took too long to come. She kept on running up the stairs until the blood was pounding through her head and she felt dizzy from the effort. She was between floors when she heard the swish of opening elevator doors just above her. If only she could reach it before they closed again. Her legs felt leaden, but she pushed them as hard as they could go. She was panting from the exertion, almost exhausted when her feet tottered on to the carpeted landing.

'Please . . .' The appeal was a bare whisper, and the man to whom she made it didn't understand. She gestured despairingly towards the elevator doors, but they were already closing behind him. It was too late.

The man said something, but there was a buzz in her ears that made his words indistinguishable. She shook her head and tried to catch her breath. The floor seemed to be spinning. 'I need help,' she gasped, frightened that she was going to faint. If she collapsed, the Arab would catch her and . . . wild, unreasoning panic scrambled her mind. She took a couple of unsteady steps.

The man grasped her arm. 'I'll get a doctor straight away.'

'No!' She looked up at him, too physically distressed to explain. There was concern in his eyes. It was a nice face, she thought, before it started swimming in front of her. She could feel the blood draining from her own and, just as her knees started to buckle, an arm came round her shoulders and another lifted her off her feet.

Her head dangled on to the broad shoulder of a pin-striped suit. A respectable, civilised suit that somehow comforted her as the man carried her along a corridor. Her torso felt as if it was wound around with hoops of steel, and a painful stitch was tearing through her abdomen. She needed to speak, but her throat was so terribly dry and the effort to do anything was too great to make.

They came to a halt. The man bent over and slid his arm from beneath her legs so she could stand up. His other arm supported her tightly against him as he fished in his pocket for a door-key. A wave of apprehension brought strength enough for Ashley to grasp some control of herself.

'I need your help,' she blurted out, 'but . . .'

He flashed her a dry, little smile. 'There will be no trouble, *mademoiselle*. I'll call a doctor for you immediately I get into my room.'

'No.' She pushed back against the door-jamb, not knowing whether to trust him or not. One nerve-shattering experience with a man was more than enough for one night and, while she still needed a means of escape, to throw herself out of a frying pan into a fire was absolute idiocy.

He shrugged his shoulders. 'I have nowhere else to take you. If you need help . . .'

His accent was heavily French. Ashley searched his face, trying to read his motives. She looked into blue-grey eyes that held the saddest expression she had ever seen.

'Of course, the door will remain open while you are here,' he asssured her. 'You may leave whenever you please.'

He could be trusted. She was suddenly very sure of it. 'Thank you,' she breathed, relieved that she had stumbled on a haven of safety.

He opened the door. She slid from the door-jamb and he caught her around the waist, steering her to the nearest armchair and lowering her into it.

'Thank you.' Her voice was even shakier than her limbs. Reaction was setting in and, fearful that the Arab might still find her, she blurted out, 'If you don't mind, I'd rather have the door closed.'

He shot her a sharp, assessing look, then moved to do her bidding. Having secured her safety he walked straight over to a side-table on which stood a bottle and a set of balloon glasses.

Ashley watched him open the bottle, then swept her gaze around the room, realising for the first time that he had brought her into one of the luxurious corner suites of the hotel. They were in a spacious sitting-room, its windows obviously overlooking the Nile as well as the square at the end of Tahrir Bridge. The furnishings were in restful shades of blue and green, and the work-manlike desk in one corner was spread with papers, suggesting that her host was in Cairo on business.

Her eyes returned to him in sharper appraisal. He was a tall man, over six foot, broad-shouldered but slim-hipped, and her recollection of a hard chest and strong muscular arms suggested he kept himself fit. His face was not young, nor was it old. It wore a settled maturity that placed him around forty, and from the lines of stress she had seen around his eyes Ashley surmised they had not all been easy years. The stylishly cut dark hair held a lot of grey.

He put down the bottle and carried a glass over to her. 'You could probably do with this,' he said, pressing it into her hand and waiting until her tremulous fingers had curled securely around it before straightening up. An enigmatic smile curved his mouth. '1906 Grande Champagne Cognac.'

'It's ... very kind of you,' Ashley murmured, suddenly feeling ill at ease with the situation. While he had certainly helped her escape from the Arab, it struck her forcibly that she didn't know this man's name either, and here she was accepting his hospitality.

She watched him warily as he drew another armchair closer to hers and sat down. He did not fully relax, but perched himself forward, elbows on the arm-rests and the fingers of one hand stroking the other.

The blue-grey eyes observed her keenly. 'You have some colour in your face now. Are you ill, or ...'

She shook her head. 'No! I was ... very ... stressed. I didn't know what to do ...' She looked at him helplessly, at a loss to put into words what had happened.

He nodded and his eyes crinkled sympathetically. 'So you have a problem. Tell me what it is and I will see what I can do to solve it.'

'A man ...' Heat flooded through her at the memory, and she took a sip of cognac in the hope of calming herself.

'You were molested?' the Frenchman asked softly.

The smooth richness of the cognac slid down her throat and she sucked in a deep breath to steady her fluttering pulse. 'No. No . . . not exactly. I . . .' Shame and her own sense of guilt would not let her accuse the Arab of taking advantage of her. 'It was the situation. It got beyond my control. I . . . I had to run away.'

She lifted agonised eyes, only to find him frowning down at the glass she held in her hand. His gaze flicked sharply up to hers. 'I was wrong to call you *mademoiselle*. You look so very young, I was deceived. But why wasn't your husband with you at this time of night? Is he without eyes, without soul?' He rose to his feet with an expression of disgust. 'I shall ring him at once to come for you.'

The old grief dragged at her heart. 'I'm alone, *m'sieur*. My husband . . . my husband is dead.'

And she remembered the torment in Damien's eyes and the despair in his soul, and she bowed her head in terrible shame for what she had done this night. Tears welled into her eyes. How could she have acted so? How could she have let that Arab get to her like that? It had been her body and the futility of wanting to satisfy all her needs that had tortured Damien into that final self-destruction.

The glass of cognac was prised out of her grasp, and through a blur of tears she saw the Frenchman looming over her. He knelt beside her chair and gently wiped her cheeks. 'Love is without mercy. It destroys everything,' he said grimly, then in a softer, more soothing tone, 'You must not weep for what is for ever gone. We will talk of other things.'

He released her hands and straightened up. His fingers brushed her cheek in a kindly gesture of encouragement. 'I don't even know your name.'

The voiced echo of her own thoughts brought a tremulous smile to her lips. 'Nor I yours.'

'Louis-Philippe de Laclos.' He gave a slight bow as he added, 'At your service.' Again his smile held a faint twist of irony, as if he expected nothing from life, least of all any pleasure.

'My name is Ashley Cunningham,' she replied, intensely grateful for the generous service he had already performed for her tonight.

He gave her a startled look, then shook his head in a bemused fashion. 'How extraordinary!'

'Why?' Ashley asked in surprise.

He gave an eloquent shrug and dropped back into his chair. His eyes roved over her features with a kind of speculative appreciation. 'I was talking to Sohaila Sha'ib this morning. MISR appointed her as my personal assistant the last time I was in Egypt, and when I saw her, naturally I stopped to pass civilities. She told me she was working with you and seemed very pleased with the assignment.'

Sohaila! Ashley rubbed at her forehead as her mind whirled. The coincidence was more extraordinary than Louis-Philippe de Laclos knew.

This whole disastrous night had started with Sohaila, the Egyptian girl's misery and Ashley's desire to help her. Then the meeting with the Arab and his offer of the money ... Ashley shuddered and forcibly dragged her mind off that insane encounter. It seemed strangely ironic that her rescuer was also connected to Sohaila.

'She mentioned something about a jewellery collection.'

Ashley grasped the prompt, needing to shift her mind on to more tangible things. 'I've been trying to organise one of the greatest collections of Egyptian jewellery ever assembled.'

'The jewellery of the Pharoahs?'

'Oh, much more than that. There's the collections of King Farouk. The Nubian silver from Aswan. The masterpieces of the Bedouins. But the Pharoahs' jewellery would certainly be the centrepiece around which the others revolved ...' She gave a weary shrug. 'That's if the Egyptian authorities will ever come to a decision about it.'

'And why can't they make up their minds?'

Ashley hesitated, but the interest in his eyes seemed genuine, not merely polite. Her own enthusiasm for the concept crept into her voice as she continued.

'To pay for the display will cost a great fortune. In order to finance the collection, the jewellery company I work for wants to sell reproductions, ranging from thousands of dollars to millions. And there's the rub, I think. It's the commercialisation that seems to worry the officials I've been talking to.'

Her eyes narrowed with determination. 'Our aim is to design and sell a fabulous range of jewellery—the Egyptian Collection—directly inspired by what I've seen here. My drawings are nearly complete. We'll cover everything from the most elaborate collars to the smallest trinkets, and I'm certain it will be successful because the pieces are so ... magnificent, so flattering to women. The Egyptians, however, wonder if we are not taking advantage of them in some devious way, even though they get a commission on everything we sell. They see the advantages in such a worldwide display in every major capital in the world ... yet still they hesitate.'

'Undoubtedly. They always do,' Louis-Philippe said with a grimace. 'They've become wary of letting anything out of the country, and it's understandable. Egypt has been plundered of so much of its treasure. That's why the restrictions are now so tight.'

He went on to describe his own experiences of working in Egypt. Ashley took further stock of the man as he talked of the difficulties in raising finance for excavations. He had been involved with many of the most productive sites that archaeologists had uncovered over the last twenty years. The cost of such long-term and labour-intensive projects had to be prohibitive. Ashley decided that Louis-Philippe de Laclos had to be on talking terms with the Rothschilds and the Rockefellers of the world.

But at least he was of her world, not like the Arab, and it was reassuring to have a calm, sane conversation that dealt with things she could comprehend. She almost felt normal again.

When the subject of antiquities lagged, she asked Louis-Philippe if he was organising some new dig. He shook his head and spoke of some restoration work in which he was presently involved. His voice used a curious range of intonation, from enthusiasm to almost a half-hearted diffidence, which suggested an ambivalent attitude towards the project.

'Isn't it going well?' she asked when his talking trailed into a heavy sigh.

His gaze lifted reluctantly and again Ashley thought they were the saddest eyes she had ever seen. His hand made an empty gesture. 'I promised myself some time ago that I would never return to Egypt. Then I made an excuse. I told myself I was needed here, but only the money was needed. I shouldn't have come.'

'Why not?' Ashley prompted curiously.

He threw her a glance that was full of self-mockery. 'They say whoever drinks from the Nile must return and taste it again. Maybe that's true, but ...' he paused and there was no humour at all in the grim smile that thinned his mouth '... along with its fascination comes too many other frustrations. The differences of race, culture, religion ... and other things ...' he shook his head '... impossible.'

The image of the Arab welled instantly into

Ashley's mind. 'Yes,' she whispered as a convulsive shiver ran down her spine.

Louis-Philippe looked sharply at her. Their eyes met and locked, and some indefinable understanding, something totally instinctive leapt between them so that they were no longer strangers apart, but people who shared the same knowledge on a level that was deeply hidden from everyone else.

'It's been good of you to give me your company for so long,' Ashley said impulsively.

'Not at all.' He smiled. 'It can be lonely in a foreign country.'

'Yes,' she agreed, pushing herself out of the armchair. 'It's very late.'

He rose swiftly to his feet. 'You must allow me to escort you to your room.'

He took her arm and Ashley did not protest the gentlemanly offer. It was almost three o'clock and although she was no longer afraid that the Arab might still be in the hotel, the security of another man's presence was very comforting. Louis-Philippe de Laclos was the type of man she should be responding to. He was kind, courtly, a real gentleman. Not like the Arab at all.

They met no one until they reached Ashley's floor. One of the room-service boys was waiting at the elevators when they stepped out. Ashley saw nothing suspicious in his presence. She did not even notice that he did not take the elevator that she and Louis-Philippe had just vacated. She was not aware that he watched them to her room, watched her press a grateful kiss on Louis-Philippe's cheek, and then took to the staircase with a hurried, stealthy step.

CHAPTER THREE

WHEN her wake-up call came in the morning, Ashley responded sluggishly, her body groaning in protest at having its rest cut short. Then the memory of last night's devastating encounter with the Arab slid into her mind and she groaned out loud.

Her abandoned response to his powerful sexuality made no sense at all. Even when she was married to Damien she had never felt so . . . so taken over. Absolutely mindless! A shaming frustration crawled through her body, sharpening the memory to a point where Ashley was goaded out of bed to seek active distraction from the feelings the Arab had aroused.

She pulled on her dressing-gown and strode out to the balcony of her room. Normally she enjoyed the view of the city stretching out to meet the desert, but this morning she winced at the noise of the traffic with its continual honking of horns, and not even the more peaceful traffic on the Nile River drew her interest.

From this height, Cairo looked like any bustling city of the modern world, but that was an illusion that had been very quickly dispelled with closer acquaintance. Two and a half thousand years ago, a Greek historian named Herodotus had written that if all the countries in the world did everything one way, then in Egypt they did it the opposite; and it still held true.

Ashley felt she had weathered the culture-shock rather well, but the whole social structure still appalled her. The restrictive rules by which women had to live were an affront to any intelligent person, yet even Sohaila accepted them, despite her rebellious stance over the marriage issue.

A knock on her door heralded the delivery of breakfast. Ashley moved swiftly through the room to admit the service-waiter. He set the tray on her table, waited for the inevitable *baksheesh* tip, then smilingly took his leave.

The continental breakfast reminded her of the strong French influence still evident in Egypt, and of the remarkable man who had been her saviour last night. Just the thought of Louis-Philippe de Laclos soothed her sense of discontent. He was a true gentleman; the kind of man she could really admire and respect.

Perhaps she would run into him again, since they were staying in the same hotel. They were both alone. She might even ask him to dine with her, as a thank-you gesture for his kindness. She would be safe with him ... safe from the mind-shattering passion aroused by the Arab.

She had to forget that experience and the feelings it had stirred, and the best way to do that was to concentrate on her work. A glance at her watch showed her that she had lingered too long over breakfast. She would be late for her appointment with Sohaila at the museum if she didn't hurry.

She quickly changed into her favourite cotton two-piece. The comfortable gored skirt and the tunic with its loose, three-quarter length sleeves were ideal for the Egyptian heat, and the bright floral pattern in red and yellow and green always gave her a buoyant feeling. She strapped on yellow sandals, and snatched up her hair brush.

There was no time to twist the long tresses into a tidy top knot. She slid side-combs into the thick waves above her ears, dashed on some lipstick, snatched up her travel-bag and sketch-folder, then scooted along to the elevators, hoping she wouldn't have too long to wait for one to come.

For once Ashley was lucky. Two minutes later she was on the front steps of the hotel and the commissionaire was waving up a taxi for her. The shiny black Mercedes surprised her. Most of the taxis in Cairo were old Volvos, scratched and dented from the daily dodgem antics of the city traffic, but she had seen a fleet of Mercedes taxis at the Meridian Hotel, so this one didn't raise any question in her mind.

The commissionaire opened the back passenger-door. Ashley was too street-wise now to step inside before an agreement had been reached on the fare. 'I want to go to the Egyptian Museum,' she said very firmly, and raised a couple of fingers in the air. 'Two pounds.'

To Ashley's relief the driver nodded, and did not bother with the usual haggling. She climbed in, feeling quite pleased with herself. A firm voice was obviously the trick to forestall argument. The commissionaire closed the door and the car moved off, smoothly joining the stream of traffic leading on to Tahrir Bridge.

Ashley relaxed into the plush leather seat,

thinking how nice a change it was from the dusty velvet upholstery in the older taxis. The whole interior of the car was spotlessly clean too, which was an even more pleasant change. She had almost become used to the prevailing dust and dirt.

One of the problems in Cairo was that it hardly ever rained, so the streets were rarely washed clean. But that didn't excuse the rubbish that was heaped up everywhere. A clean-up programme was badly needed. It was a terrible shame, the way some things were just let go. There were so many beautiful things in this city, like the gorgeous poinciana trees ...

Ashley's attention drifted to those blooming along the bank of the Nile, and she was too late to stop the driver from taking a wrong turn down to Garden City. She leant forward and tapped his shoulder. 'The Egyptain Museum. It's not this way. You have to go back through Tahrir Square,' she explained in irritation. If he thought he was going to take her for more than two pounds, he could think again. She wasn't a green tourist.

The driver nodded, but he didn't turn back. Ashley was about to tap him again when she realised they were in a one-way street. She settled back with a sigh of exasperation. The whole damned traffic-system was a maze of one-way streets, and once the wrong one was selected it was the devil of a job to get back on course again.

She checked her watch. It was already ten o'clock. She was going to be late and Sohaila was always punctual. That was something the Egyptian authorities had got right, Ashley thought on a sigh of general vexation. Sohaila worked for MISR, the government agency which kept tabs on Ashley's work in Egypt, and from the very beginning she had been a goldmine of information, knowing precisely where to find what Ashley wanted, and capable of giving her all the background detail she needed. They had very quickly formed a good working relationship, and over the weeks they had spent together, a close friendship had grown between them.

Ashley wished she could have won the money last night. It would have been marvellous to hand it to Sohaila this morning and see excitement replace the dull misery in the lovely expressive eyes. If only she had had the luck of the Arab! He had boasted that he always won. Well, he hadn't won with her, Ashley thought, but it had been too near a thing to feel anything but a hollow triumph.

The Mercedes slowed down and the driver pulled over to the kerb. They were nowhere near the museum. With a stab of annoyance Ashley leaned forward to instruct the driver again, but just as she was about to speak the passenger-door was opened and a man in Arabic dress pushed into the seat beside her, slamming the door behind him.

Ashley's heart did a quick somersault, but it wasn't the Arab of last night. 'This is my taxi. You get out this minute or I'll call the tourist police,' she blustered angrily.

The man was completely unmoved. Hard, dark eyes gave her only a cursory glance as the Mercedes moved off again.

'Stop!' Ashley cried out, but the driver took no notice of her. Fear fluttered through her stomach.

She turned back to the Arab. 'You have no right ...'

'Calm yourself, *madame*,' he said in precise English. 'No harm will come to you. The Sheikh requires your presence. That is all.'

'That's all!' Ashley heard her voice climb to a shrill note and quickly sucked in a deep breath. Her heart hammered around her chest. The Sheikh! The Arab with the golden corded *'iqal*. He was having her abducted. Right off the steps of the Sheraton Hotel!

Fool! Fool! Fool! she railed at herself for not realising that such a man would never accept defeat. She should have been anticipating some follow-up to last night's confrontation. Hadn't he said she couldn't escape him? And this was his answer to her vehement rejection. He was not giving her any choice in the matter. He was taking, with ruthless disregard for her right to make her own decisions. And where did that disregard stop? Would it stop at all?

CHAPTER FOUR

ASHLEY tried her utmost to stave off panic. The situation would have been incredible if it wasn't so horribly real. Abducted! In broad daylight!

'He can't get away with this!' she cried in outrage, and turned to the Arab beside her, her voice rising in bitter protest. 'There are laws in this country!'

The response she got was even more nerve-shattering. 'The Sheikh is beyond the law, *madame*. You are honoured to be asked ...'

'Asked! I wasn't asked!' Ashley almost shrieked.

'That is immaterial.' The black eyes he turned to her held no grain of sympathy for her plight. 'Please do no attempt anything foolish. It would be my duty to restrain you. The Sheikh does not want you hurt in any way, so there is no need for you to be concerned. Relax, *madame*. Our journey will not be long.'

It was impossible for Ashley to relax. The memory of the man's air of ruthless power was all too vivid. Hadn't she even thought last night that he was capable of killing to get what he wanted? She had been the worst possible fool to have challenged such a person.

The Mercedes was halted by traffic and Ashley lunged for the door handle, desperate to escape.

She pressed it frantically, but the door did not open.

'The locks are power-controlled, *madame*. Please do not distress yourself. It will change nothing.'

The words beat on her fevered brain like inexorable drums of doom. The man beside her might not wish to use force, but he was certainly strong enough to subdue any struggle she might put up. The wisest course was probably to sit back and concentrate hard on the streets they were passing. If she could memorise the route, it might be of some use to her.

Her eyes darted from side to side, picking up every landmark possible. She did not recognise anything and did not know where they were until she spotted the distinctive minaret and huge walls of Ibn Tulun's Mosque, built over a thousand years ago, and still the largest mosque in Cairo. They had to be near the medieval part of the old city, not so very far from the business centre, and only half a kilometre from the Australian and British embassies.

Minutes later, the Mercedes turned into a narrow street, hardly more than an alley, compelling the driver to slow the car to a crawl. He threaded a path between the buildings before entering a gateway. Ashley caught only a glimpse of a formidable, two-storied stone building, bisected at ground level by the cobbled road.

The car drew to a halt in front of the steps which led into a side-entrance of the building. The driver got out, opened the door on her side, then stood guard next to it.

This private cul-de-sac gave Ashley no possible chance of escape. With a despondent sigh, she allowed herself to be handed out, and then followed the Arab into the entrance hall of the building. It was perfectly clear that putting up a fight could only end in her being hurt, perhaps badly.

The two men, one on each side of Ashley, took her along a screened corridor to a central courtyard. Resistance seemed futile, but beyond the fear that Ashley felt was a mounting anger against the man who had ordered this outrageous action, this violation of her right as a person to make her own choices.

They mounted a flight of stairs, at the head of which were a pair of double doors. One of the men flung them open, and gestured for Ashley to proceed. She entered a huge *qa'ah*, or reception room, which took up two floors of the building. At either end were two great *liwans*. The galleries along both sides were fronted with *mishrabiyyah* screens, an arabesque wooden filigree behind which anyone could watch the activity below. In the centre of an ornate marble floor was a beautiful mosaic fountain.

A woman appeared, garbed in the traditional black gown, her face covered with a veil. The Arab addressed her in a tone of command. 'Escort *madame* to the harim and see that she has refreshments.' Then he turned to Ashley. 'I trust you will be comfortable there, *madame*. The Sheikh will attend you as soon as he is free.'

He pronounced the word sheikh in the Arabic way, with a guttural 'k', harsh and discordant, yet Ashley heard the subservience in his voice and could see the respect in his manner. It was the goad that spurred anger beyond fear. She had no reason to respect the man who had forced her here; and subservience was the last reaction he was going to get from her. How dared he think he could place her in his 'harim' in this overly exotic place?

There was no point in being passive any longer. If it meant getting hurt, then that was better than tamely waiting on any Sheikh's pleasure. The two men turned to leave, and the woman-servant took Ashley by the arm.

'Oh, no, you don't!' Ashley cried striking the restraining hand away and stepping out of reach.

The men halted and looked back at her in surprise. The woman hesitated a moment. Instinctively drawing on all her experience in Egypt, Ashley threw her head up haughtily, assumed an expression of command and stamped her foot. She slapped her hands vehemently together and shouted '*La! La! La!*' which was the Arabic for 'no'.

The woman stared at Ashley in mesmerised uncertainty. Having won this momentary advantage, Ashley turned to the men, and yelled her orders. 'Go to your Sheikh immediately! Tell him I will not be put in anyone's "harim". And if you so much as try it, I promise you'll all get more trouble than anyone ever bargained for.'

She sucked in a quick breath and continued the tirade with barely a pause. 'And if it's pleasure he wants, I doubt that it will serve his purpose to have me bruised and beaten, so you'd better not lay a finger on me. In fact, I'm walking out of here right now, and don't you try to stop me. You go and tell your master that!'

Ashley started walking towards the door. The men glanced at each other, apprehension and indecision reflected in their expressions. 'Go! Go!' Ashley yelled at them, gesticulating wildly in the hope it might help.

Suddenly the woman snatched hold of Ashley's upper arm and tugged at it, not very hard, but insistently. It was more than Ashley could tolerate. For all her bravado she was trembling inside, and her reaction to this form of coercion was instant and violent. She shook herself free and pushed the woman away with all her strength.

Taken unawares, the woman stumbled backwards, lost her footing on the edge of the fountain and collapsed with a cry into a spray of water. Ashley stood paralysed on the spot, wondering what would happen to her now. A gabble of Arabic broke forth from the men, louder than the wail of distress from the fountain; but the sound that shook Ashley most of all was the soft, male laughter echoing down from behind the *mashrabiyyah* in the galleries.

Her head jerked up, eyes darting around the

meshed screen, her mind leaping into even more feverish turmoil. He had been watching her; enjoying the fact that she was powerless to escape him this time, and amused by her attempt to assert her independence. Ashley seethed over her impotence, and wildly vowed that she would make his triumph over her a bitter one. She would fight him with every weapon at her disposal.

The laughter suddenly stopped. Terse commands followed in Arabic, but Ashley's knowledge of the language was too sketchy to understand them. She was sure of only one thing. They were not meant for her well-being.

The woman hurriedly waded out of the fountain, gathering up her wet skirts and wringing the water from them as she did so. She bowed to Ashley and scuttled off to an exit at the back of the room. The two men also bowed, then took a more dignified exit through the double doorway. The doors closed behind them with an ominous clang.

For a moment she was alone, but Ashley did not doubt that the Sheikh was on his way to her and any attempt to use either exit would be thwarted. At least she had shown him she had a mind of her own and would not be tamely installed in any damned harim'!

However, that small victory was little consolation to her as she thought how she might be tamed after the way she had reacted to him last night. She had to do something more concrete to protect herself from him.

She forced herself to move, so that he would not

find her waiting like a mesmerised rabbit. She skirted the fountain, trying to put more distance between herself and the door she expected him to enter by. If she kept the water between them he couldn't touch her. Unless he forced his will on her in the fountain. Ashley shuddered.

Her eye caught an ornamental scimitar hanging high up on the end wall. The downward turning handle was elaborately carved and studded with gem-stones. The long blade curved wickedly upwards in its scabbard. It was exactly what she wanted.

This Arab sheikh was not the kind of man to call for help in a confrontation with a woman. It would be beneath his pride. So perhaps she could hold him at bay with this weapon, or at least make some stand that would induce him to think twice about what he was doing. Driven by a sense of urgency, Ashley leapt upon an adjacent divan, and reached up to lift the scimitar out of its holder, hoping that the blade was not entirely useless.

The ease with which it ran from its scabbard surprised her. Light flashed from the blade as she stepped down. A few testing slashes gave her a feel for the perfect balance, and Ashley no longer had any doubt that she held a very formidable weapon. For the first time this morning she had some control of the situation.

'Take care. That sword is said to have belonged to Salah al-Din. It's made from the finest Damascene steel, the best the world has ever known.'

Ashley wheeled around to face her tormentor. 'It means I'll run you through with it before I'll let you get away with this!' she fired at him.

He laughed. He was just as she remembered him, the amused arrogance on his face barely lightening his air of ruthless purpose.

'I don't care who you think you are,' Ashley bit out angrily, determined not to be intimidated by his manner, 'but as far as I'm concerned you're not above the law, and I'll defend myself to your death.'

There was a fleeting glint of admiration in his eyes before his face sobered into hard command. 'You have courage. I respect you for it, if for nothing else. However, you obviously do not understand your position. I can do with you as I wish. And I will. The sword means nothing.' He paused so that his next statement would have its maximum effect. 'The law cannot touch me. In this country I have diplomatic immunity.'

He walked around the fountain as he spoke, approaching her with all the confidence of a man who knew he was untouchable. His smile was cruel. 'Whereas you, Mrs Cunningham, would bring upon yourself a most unenviable fate if you injure me in any way. A far more disagreeable fate than any you'll meet here with me.'

Ashley gulped, but defiance still spat off her tongue. 'When it's known what you have done to me you will be expelled from the country. The authorities will ...'

'Perhaps,' he shrugged. 'But it will be worth it!'

'Why are you doing this to me?'

His eyes mocked her. 'You are an intelligent woman. A clever woman. Or you would not have been sent here by the firm of Dewar and Buller to negotiate with the authorities over a collection of jewellery. Such a mission requires some finesse in judgement. It would be a very stupid, self-defeating move to use that sword *madame*. Give it to me and I shall return it to where it belongs.'

He stepped up against the point of the blade. Ashley held firm, all too aware that any retreat would show weakness. He pressed forward, letting the sword prick his chest and a drop of blood stained the pure white cashmere of his tunic. Their eyes locked, his challenging, hers frantically defiant.

'Or use it as you wish,' he said quietly.

Whatever the rights or the wrongs of the situation, Ashley knew she could not hurt or kill the man in cold blood. And his logic was impeccable. He had shaken her resolve with each point he had made. The fact that he had learnt so much about her in so little time confirmed his position of power, and the inside of an Egyptian jail would leave her with no options at all.

When he reached for the sword, Ashley did nothing to stop him from taking it. She was defeated, and they both knew it. Her fingers felt nerveless as she loosened her grip. He balanced the sword in both hands, and again his mouth curved into that cruel smile. His black eyes stared into hers, completely merciless.

'What a pity that you are not as fine a work of art as the sword. Or as constant. This blade can cut the finest silk with a mere stroke.'

Ashley blazed defiance back at him. 'And you're just like it—a relic from the past! The twentieth century hasn't even touched you.' She swept a contemptuous gaze over the rich, Ottoman furnishings of the room. 'You even live like some great Khan of long ago.'

He gave a sardonic laugh. 'This house was restored and furnished by an English general who fancied the surroundings of oriental splendour while he exercised his more sophisticated pleasures with Nubian boys. But, of course, you would not find that kind of behaviour at all reprehensible, would you?'

Ashley was shocked and confused by his savage counter-attack. 'Yes, I would,' she insisted, instinctively rising the the taunt.

His mouth curled again. 'You surprise me, Mrs Cunningham. Don't you take your pleasure when and how you please, without regard for anyone but yourself?'

Ashley was so stunned by the accusation that he had turned away before she found wits enough to form an answer. 'That's not true,' she croaked, her throat completely dry from a resurgence of fear. If he believed that of her, she didn't have much chance of persuading him to let her go free.

He ignored her, returning the sword to its position on the wall with a careful reverence that suggested it meant more to him than anything she might say.

Ashley swallowed hard. She only had words left to defend herself. 'You have no right to judge me like that. How dare you assume . . .'

'I don't assume.' He turned, a taut grimness sharpening the hard planes of his face. 'I know! Cairo is one of the meeting places of the world, and in my position I have information available to me that is not available to others. I now know that you're a married woman, but you have no sense of fidelity. Last night you wanted me. Only fear stopped you.'

He paused, and an acid note crept into the flat, emotionless tone. 'You went straight from me to another man. After some considerable time, enough time to satisfy your . . . needs, he returned you to your room, where you gave him a loving farewell before he left. The man was not your husband.'

His indictment of her behaviour was like a series of punches that almost knocked Ashley off her feet. She rallied slowly, attacking him in blind self-defence. 'So this is the justification for your actions, is it? I hurt your monumental ego, so you resort to force to get what you want.'

'I took a short-cut, yes. A quick means to an end, but the end will not require any force, will it, Ashley? I would not want to use it, and I will not have to.'

The absolute assurance in that soft, personal taunt sent a shiver of uncertainty down her spine.

The memory of her response to him last night throbbed between them, undeniable. And he was evoking a response in her even now, just by looking at her with that mocking challenge in his hard, black eyes.

Her long neck stiffened as his gaze raked the rippling silkiness of her hair to where it fell loosely over her shoulders. When his eyes dropped lower, her breasts tingled with awareness, their nipples jutting hard against the flimsy nylon bra and cotton tunic. A trembling weakness invaded her thighs and by the time he returned his gaze to hers, Ashley was dredging desperately for the strength to fight his devastating effect on her.

'You think you know everything, but you know nothing!' she snapped at him.

'Is it easier for you to deceive yourself than to see the truth?'

'You haven't got the faintest inkling about what kind of person I am,' she retorted hotly.

'I don't care!' he said with a savagery that silenced her, and desire blazed from his eyes, so fiercely intense that it engulfed Ashley, shrivelling every line of defence in her mind.

He stepped forward and curved his hand around her cheek and chin. His voice dropped to a low, riveting note of passion. 'I don't care if you've had a thousand men, because they haven't had you, Ashley. They haven't reached inside you and twisted your gut so that you can't think of anything but the man who's possessing you and how that feels. And I intend for you to feel that. With me. I don't care what words you spout, because I know ...'

His thumb moved, brushing slowly over her lower lip. '... I know that you will surrender to me, Ashley Cunningham. Body and soul.'

Her heart was thundering in her chest, wildly protesting the sheer sexual force of the man. Her mind groped desperately for something, anything to repel this insidious attack on the very core of her being. 'I loved my husband. I loved him,' she whispered with hoarse vehemence, the old pain swimming into her eyes. 'And he killed himself because he loved me. Do you think you could ever take his place in my heart?'

It gave her a fierce satisfaction to see the fire of passion recoil behind the narrowed blackness of his eyes. His hand tightened its grip around her face. His lips thinned in some inner conflict. She sensed the wave of violence that he fought back before he dropped his hand and turned away from her with a sharp, angry abruptness.

He paced across the room like a man driven with scourges, but when he wheeled around, his face was completely expressionless. 'So ... you are a widow,' he said coldly.

'Yes.' She felt too depleted of energy to say more.

'Tell me how your husband died.'

A shudder ran through her and Ashley tried to control the revulsion she felt at his callous command. 'It's none of your business,' she replied flatly, fighting the tears that pricked at her eyes.

Pride insisted that she should show no weakness in front of him.

'Ashley, I am giving you the chance to explain yourself, and I will not brook defiance.'

Something inside her snapped from all the tension he had put her through. 'Go to hell!' she screamed at him, and the tears could not be contained any longer. They streamed down her face and she could do nothing to stop them. 'I don't care what you think of me,' she sobbed. 'I don't care what you do to me. Take what you want! It won't be much, I promise you. Just get it over with and let me go.'

He crossed the room in a few strides, grasped her upper arms with fingers of steel, and roughly shook her until her head was flung back and she sobbed helplessly.

'You cannot escape me like this,' he exploded in fury. 'This is one of your tricks. However much you say you loved your husband, he's dead. He's dead and you're alive, and I felt your heart beating with mine last night, so don't tell me it's lying in a grave with him.'

'You don't understand,' she choked out.

'Then tell me!'

Tears kept spilling down her cheeks as she flung the words at him. 'He had a ... a wasting disease ...' She couldn't say it. Her mind sheered away from that horror and tried another path. 'It was making his body ... useless. He couldn't be the man he was. Not with me. We couldn't have children. It wasn't the pain that drove him to ...

to end his life. It was ... me. It was because of me!'

The terrible guilt which had burdened her heart suddenly burst from her. 'The sight of me tortured him. He wanted me to have a normal life ... and we couldn't. Not any more. I wanted him ... just to hold me. To let me hold him. But he hated not being able to ... be what he was ...'

She lifted agonised eyes to the darkly brooding man who had demanded so much from her, then plunged on to the last haunting grief. 'That last night ... he kissed me. He kissed me all over. And when I went to sleep, he went out ... and shot himself. So you see, I haven't wanted ... any ... not any man since ... Damien died. And I certainly don't want you! I don't know why I reacted to you last night. I'm sorry. It was wrong. It was ...'

'No!'

She lifted sad, empty eyes. 'I don't know you.'

His gaze was hard and insistent, but his hands gentled their hold, then slid up to cup her face. 'The Baron de Laclos. What about him?' he demanded.

'The Baron?' She felt too drained to think. The pain that had been dragged to the surface still clouded her mind. 'Do you mean Louis-Philippe?'

'The man you ran to last night,' he said harshly.

Her eyes were empty of interest and she replied with some difficulty, groping for the right words to explain. 'A ... a friend. I was upset and he helped me. He showed me kindness when I needed it. He's a good man.'

A long sigh whispered from his lips and the harshness melted from his face. An ironic smile curved the strong, sensual mouth. 'A pity, perhaps, that I cannot be kind, but that wouldn't work for me, would it?'

Ashley couldn't follow his meaning. 'It never hurts to be kind.'

'Then will you be so . . . to me?'

The soft appeal was so unexpected that it confused Ashley. She stared up at him, struggling to understand what this abrupt change of manner meant.

'Stay here as my guest.'

'And if I don't want to stay?' she pleaded.

He stroked her cheek in a softly mocking salute as he released her. 'I'm afraid I cannot give you any choice in the matter. Until the course has been run.'

CHAPTER FIVE

WHAT course? He was speaking in riddles. Or *was* he? Ashley lifted her hand to her cheek, unconsciously rubbing at the warmth his palm had left there. She felt drained. Her mind was sluggish, revolving in slow, heavy circles without grasping anything clearly. There was no longer any threat in his manner, and yet ... until the course has been run ...

He still meant to have her!

And she had nothing to fight him with any more. Nothing! With a little cry of despair she turned her back on him and forced her legs to carry her to the divan. She sank on to the cushions and slowly lifted bleak eyes to her nemesis.

'Why mince words? I'm not your guest. I'm your prisoner.'

He came and sat beside her, taking her hand and fondling it with a gentleness that surprised her. 'You will have the freedom of the house. There is no reason why you cannot be ... comfortable here. And you have my word that I will not take from you anything you don't wish to give.'

'I don't wish to give you anything!' she retorted bitterly. 'Let me have my freedom. There's no point in your keeping me here. I shall never forgive you for what you've done.'

His gaze dropped to her hand and his thumb pushed savagely at her rings, causing the diamond solitaire to dig into her middle finger. 'What's done cannot be undone,' he muttered, then lifted eyes that held a strangely moving intensity. 'I cannot let you go. You must accept that, Ashley.'

Her mind screamed no, even as her body turned traitor and yearned for a reawakening of the passion which had flared between them last night. Ashley tore her gaze from his, averting her head so that he could not reach her with those compelling eyes. The painful thump of her heart was reminder enough of the way he could affect her.

'I could never love you,' she whispered, then realised with jolting horror that the words concealed much that she meant to remain hidden.

For several long moments he made no answer, and his silence held a tension that played havoc with her ragged nerves.

'My name is Azir,' he finally murmured. 'Azir Talil Khaybar.'

A ripple of panic cramped Ashley's stomach. She did not want to know his name. Somehow it made him a person instead of a cruel, ruthless tyrant who would stop at nothing to get his own way. She had to remember that. It was impossible to yield to the temptation he was offering. That would justify what he had done to her, and she would never, never give him that satisfaction.

'Why do I disturb you so much?'

The soft question jangled her frayed emotions even further. She didn't understand it herself.

Why him? Of all the men she had met since Damien's death, why was it this man who had roused feelings that were shaming her even now?

'Look at me, Ashley!' he commanded.

She couldn't resist. Without any conscious volition, her head turned towards him, her inner conflict still mirrored in her eyes.

He reached up and removed the head-dress. His hair was black and straight, its thickness slightly rumpled. Somehow it made him look more human, not quite so invincible, but the glint of triumph burning in his black eyes warned her that any suggestion of humanity should be instantly discounted.

'I'm not a man who makes decisions lightly, or acts without a strong foundation on which to build. I've handled top-level negotiations for my country for many years.' He paused a moment to give emphasis to his coming words. 'We have something too strong between us to ...'

'No!' she denied vehemently, driven by his certainty to strike an even more certain wedge between them. I could never be happy with a man who only wants me for ... for physical gratification. You've given me a forceful demonstration of how little you regard the rights of women.'

'If I had no regard for you I would not be talking now, when every instinct I have is crying out with my need ... for you.'

His gaze dropped to her mouth and again Ashley jerked her head away, biting her lips to prevent any tell-tale quiver. 'You'll get nothing from me,' she cried back at him. 'Nothing,'

'Time will prove or disprove that,' he replied, and the relentless purpose in his voice sent a cold chill down her spine.

In sheer desperation she pleaded with him. 'Let me go. I won't report any of this to the police if you'll just let me go.'

'That is impossible.'

He was hell-bent on the course of destruction he had chosen, and there seemed no way of shifting him from it, but Ashley still could not accept the inevitable end. She stared down at the richly woven Persian carpet on the floor. It pictured the Tree of Life. She grimly wondered where *her* life was heading now.

'You simply don't care how this will affect me, do you?' she observed, deriding herself for the futility of the words even as she spoke them.

'Perhaps I care too much,' he suggested softly.

She flashed him a look of scathing disbelief, but again she was caught and confused by the dark intensity of his eyes. 'You brought me here to violate me,' she accused, more from the need to remind herself of that fact than to recall it to his notice.

'Did I?' He let the question hang between them for several seconds before he added, 'You said you hadn't fully understood the desperation your husband felt. Obviously you're unaware of the effect you can have on a man. In his position, I would have done the same as he.'

He lifted her hand and pressed it to the

bloodstain on his tunic. The strong heartbeat under her palm seemed to vibrate through her own body and she recoiled from the contact as if she had been burnt, snatching her hand away and hugging it under her other arm. 'How dare you cite my husband in defence of your own actions?' she hissed at him. 'How dare you compare your . . . your lust to Damien's love?'

His face hardened. She sensed the firming of his purpose even before he spoke, but the words cut straight to her heart with devastating force.

'He's dead, Ashley. And on your own admission, you've been dead to any feeling too. Until we met last night. Don't tell me you want to crawl back into the grave with him.'

He rose from the divan, and with a sharp, angry gesture, paced away from her. When he wheeled around, his whole demeanour was one of arrogant command. 'As for what I dare . . . I dare anything that will keep you with me. You can fight me with whatever weapons you like, and for as long as you like—but I will not let you go.'

Shock drove Ashley to her feet. Her hands fluttered an appeal even as a protest leapt off her tongue. 'You can't mean . . .' She licked lips which were suddenly parched dry. 'You can't mean you want to keep me here . . . for ever?'

'You will live with me,' he said unequivocally.

She swallowed hard. 'You intend to imprison me in this house for the rest of my life?' Her voice came out as a frightened squeak.

'Of course not! I have to travel to many

different countries and you will come with me wherever I go. But for the present we stay here.'

'You can't do this!' she shrilled.

'It is an easy matter to have your passport re-registered with the police.'

Her mind clutched frantically at straws. 'The airport authorities ...'

'Do not look at my private jet.'

'The firm I work for ... who sent me here ... they'll ask questions ...'

'You will not be the first missing person who cannot be traced.'

'Why? Why?' she repeated helplessly.

'Because I want you,' came the relentless answer.

Ashley took a deep breath to ease the constriction in her chest. It was hard to believe what he was saying, yet he left her with no doubt that he meant every word. 'I'll fight you every inch of the way,' she promised him bitterly.

'Then so be it,' he retorted, his tone as Arctic as an immovable glacier. 'Perhaps by tonight you will have had time to re-assess the situation, and your mood will not be quite so intractable. I will have you shown to your room.'

He was already striding past the fountain before Ashley snapped out of her shocked daze. 'Azir!' she cried after him in total desperation.

He paused and turned an impassive face towards her.

Somehow she had to reach into him, show him the inevitable end to what he was doing. Her hands lifted in one more appeal. 'Can't you see how hopeless it is? There is too much that is different between us.'

Slowly he swung around and for once he showed her compassion. His voice dropped to a softer tone, begging her understanding. 'I am not a fool, Ashley. I see almost insurmountable obstacles that have to be overcome for you and me to be happy together. I know I will grieve people who are very dear to me because I choose to have you at my side. But I cannot ... will not give up hope that what I want with you will be realised. Given time.'

She shook her head in helpless despair. 'It's not the kind of life I want.' Then, in bitter frustration at his immovable stance, she hurled more defiance at him. 'At the first opportunity I get I'll escape from whatever prison you try to keep me in, Azir. And I will not be put in your damned harim!'

'Do you think I want it to be like this between us?' he retorted fiercely, thrusting his hand out in angry supplication. 'What choice do you leave me?'

And while Ashley was still digesting his out-burst of frustration, Azir wheeled away and strode to the end of the room. He flung open the door through which he had entered, and clapped his hands sharply.

'Heba!'

A young Egyptian girl came running. She wore a light blue yashmak, but her face was uncovered and on it was written an anxious desire to please.

She bowed to her master and then to Ashley.

'Heba, you will look after Mrs Cunningham. Show her to the Damascus Room. See to everything she wants or needs. I will be seriously displeased if you fail me in any way.'

He turned briefly to Ashley and the tone of voice was lethally matter-of-fact. 'You will find our security here more than adequate. I know how to guard my possessions. Don't waste your time in futile thoughts or actions, Ashley.'

Then he was gone, leaving her alone with the servant-girl. Ashley did not move. Fear was ballooning through her mind and it took every shred of will-power to contain it. A fit of hysterics was not going to help her out of this situation. She didn't know if anything could, but if there was any possible line of escape she had to find it.

'*Madame*?' The Egyptian girl gestured towards the door. 'It is this way.'

The way to the Damascus Room ... that was what the girl meant ... but was there a way out? And the girl ... could her sympathies be worked upon? Ashley's mind was working feverishly as she walked down the room. She forced a smile. 'Your name is Heba?'

The smile returned was full of ingenuous pleasure. 'Yes, *madame*.'

'It's a very lovely name. Have you been in service here very long?' Ashley quizzed, hoping the girl's sense of loyalty was not very deep.

Puzzlement flitted over the young face. The girl

could only be sixteen or seventeen. An impression-able age, Ashley hoped.

'I have always lived here, *madame*. My family . . . we look after the house.' The smile lit up again. 'The Damascus Room is beautiful. You will like it very much.'

Ashley sighed. It was highly doubtful that the girl could be persuaded into any action that would adversely affect her family, but it still had to be tried if all else failed. Reserving comment, Ashley followed Heba out of the *qa'ah*, along a corridor, up a flight of stairs, and along another corridor. The house was a veritable maze and it was obvious that finding her way to an exit was not going to be easy without help.

In some other situation, Ashley would have found the Damascus Room fascinating. The lacquered walls and ceiling with their gilding and intricate patterns deserved closer study, as did the ornate carving of the Islamic furniture. The rugs on the floor were stunningly beautiful and every fabric in the furnishings was a richly woven work of art. But Ashley moved straight to the window, sweeping the curtains aside without any regard for the heavy silk.

Beyond the glass was an iron grille, barring her way to freedom. The fear billowed anew and Ashley fought it down. 'Are all the windows in the house barred, Heba?' she asked, straining to keep her voice steady.

'Yes, *madame*. It is for safety. No one can get

in, except through the doors.'

Or get out, Ashley thought despairingly. And such grilles weren't at all unusual in Cairo. She had seen them on a lot of private houses, as well as official residences. 'How many doors are there? I mean, for coming to or going from the house.'

'There are the entrance doors where you came in, *madame*, and the door to the kitchens. But these are always guarded. The Sheikh ... he is a very important man. He has to be protected,' she added in a tone of reverence.

And there would be no way past his hand-picked guards, Ashley concluded. For a few moments she was swamped by the hopelessness of her position and it took an enormous effort to pull herself together. She couldn't afford to give in to despair. That would only sap her will to fight, and fight she had to, or accept defeat ... a whole life of defeat as a second-class citizen in Azir's world. A prisoner of his will and desires.

She turned back to the girl. 'Heba, I would like a cup of tea. Is that possible?'

'Of course, *madame*. Anything you want is possible. It is the Sheikh's orders. I will go and get it for you.'

Left alone, Ashley paced the floor, driving her mind to look at the possibilities of rescue. However remote they were, it was better to think positively than allow fear to take over. And even worse than the fear was the insidious fascination ... the temptation to even think that she might like what this man intended to do to her. That had to be blocked out of her mind at all costs. She had to concentrate all her efforts on escaping.

It was now almost midday. Would Sohaila have gone to the hotel looking for her when the appointment at the museum had not been kept? Sohaila would have been puzzled, hesitant about pursuing enquiries in case Ashley had been called out on other business. Even if she had gone to MISR and reported Ashley's absence, would anything be done? Undoubtedly the Sheikh would have covered that contingency, anyway. He had known all about why she was in Egypt.

The Australian embassy? Would anyone there remark on her failure to keep up contacts? Not for a few days. If then. They probably wouldn't act until an enquiry came from her firm in Sydney, and it could be weeks before anyone back home would be disturbed by her continued silence. She might not even be in Egypt by the time someone started looking for her.

No one even knew that she had met an Arab sheikh. A man . . . that was all she had told Louis-Philippe de Laclos last night, and their acquaintance was so slight that the Baron de Laclos would not find her disappearance notable. A rueful smile flitted over her mouth. A Baron, no less. Born and bred a gentleman. But there was no hope of his helping her out of this situation.

Ashley shook her head despondently and slumped down on the bed. A double bed. And tonight . . . the hell of it was, she wasn't sure that

Azir Talil Khaybar wouldn't get exactly what he
wanted from her. When he had kissed her last
night she had had no control over her reaction.
None at all. And even this morning he had still
evoked a sexual awareness that she didn't understand—or want.

Somehow she had to keep warding him off. He
didn't want to use force and Ashley didn't think
he would. He had promised . . . but how much did
a promise mean to such a man? If she didn't
weaken as he expected her to, would his pride
demand some redress?

Ashley's frenzied thoughts were interrupted by
Heba's return with a tea-tray, set with Spode
china. For one treacherous moment Ashley wondered how she would like being the cosseted
mistress of a man who could afford Spode china
and a private jet, but her soul instantly rebelled
against the physical servitude that would be
demanded of her. She could not give in to him
tonight. If she could hold out . . . an opportunity
for escape had to come. Had to!

Once again Ashley quelled an upsurge of panic
and set herself to winning the Egyptian girl's
confidence. She poured out her cup of tea and,
under the guise of natural interest in her surroundings, she proceeded to question the girl
about the plan of the house. Heba was only too
happy to tell her all about it; the wonderful
library, the English dining-room, and all the other
rooms, including the 'harim', which was not what
Ashley had imagined at all.

'That is the room for the Sheikh's wife,' Heba explained, 'so she can do as she pleases. It is where she would meet and talk with her lady guests, just as the *qa'ah* is where the men guests are entertained.'

Ashley's sense of outrage returned in full measure. Azir Talil Khaybar was not only abusing her, but also his wife! Ashley hadn't even thought about whether he was married or not. He had swamped all normal thoughts with an intensity of feeling that had blotted out the possibility of there being any other woman in his life.

'Where is his wife?' Ashley asked, the outrage suddenly deflating into a hurt, hollow feeling.

Heba looked surprised at the question. 'The Sheikh is not married.'

Ashley felt bewildered. 'But you said that the harim . . .'

'I only meant that is its traditional purpose,' Heba explained.

Ashley was conscious of a very positive feeling of relief. Not that Azir's single status changed her position at all. She was still his prisoner.

'If you would like, I will show it to you,' Heba suggested eagerly. 'We are in the women's quarters of the house so we will not disturb anyone, and it is a very beautiful room.'

To Heba, every room in the house was very beautiful. Ashley doubted that the girl could see any fault in anything that the Sheikh owned, or did. However, there might be some advantage in seeing the layout of the women's quarters, so

Ashley quickly agreed to the girl's suggestion.

The 'harim' was luxurious with its rich sofas and armchairs, elaborately carved coffee-tables and magnificent Persian rugs. Excited by being able to show off such splendour, Heba started to giggle as she demonstrated that a corner cupboard was not a cupboard at all, but a secret room from where the ladies could watch the men's entertainment below in the *qa'ah*.

It barely measured six foot by six, but it contained two upholstered stools and the *mashrabiyyah* screen allowed a good view of any activity below. Ashley looked across at the gallery on the other side of the *qa'ah* from where the laughter had come this morning. 'What's over there?' she enquired.

'Oh, that is part of the men's quarters,' was the dismissive reply.

'I'd like to see everything,' Ashley pressed.

Heba retreated in some fluster. 'No. No! It is not permitted. You may only see the women's quarters.'

And so much for the freedom of the house, Ashley thought bitterly.

Heba beckoned her out of the secret room and hastily shut the door, her young face stamped with concern over whether she had committed an indiscretion in revealing its existence. She gestured to a table on the other side of the 'harim'. 'Would you like to sit here, *madame*? It is nice for lunch. You can see the roof garden.'

Through grilled windows, Ashley observed, but

she accepted the suggestion. Poor Heba was weighed down with the responsibility of trying to please her; and it was better than looking at a bed, which reminded her all too forcefully of what might happen tonight.

Lunch was savoury meatballs and rice, cooked in the Egyptian style, and accompanied by the usual elaborate salad. Ashley had no appetite for any food, but she mananged to force some of it down. The time was rapidly coming when she would need all her strength.

It did not sit well on her churning stomach. A clammy perspiration beaded her forehead, and she had to ask Heba to take her to the bathroom. The girl was distressed when Ashley finally vomited, apologising profusely and wringing her hands as if she was frightened of being blamed for the sickness.

It had nothing to do with Heba or the food. The emotional turmoil caused by this morning's traumatic events was taking its toll, but it seemed futile to explain that. Heba would not understand and Ashley felt too physically drained to try talking about it. She didn't even protest when Heba steered her back to the Damascus Room and insisted she lie down.

The girl fussed over her, washing her face and arms with iced water before running from the room in order to bring back some new remedy which might help. The application of smelling salts nearly choked Ashley before she realised what was being offered. Another meal was prepared and brought to her, but Ashley could only wave it away uneaten.

Heba's desperation and terror concerning the welfare of her charge finally communicated itself to Ashley, but nothing she could say or do appeared to calm the girl. Heba was frantically worried that there might be something seriously wrong, and continued to fuss until Ashley could bear it no longer.

'Heba, please ... just go away and leave me alone!' she demanded irritably.

But Heba would not go. She had to stay by her mistress. That was the order of the Sheikh.

It was the last straw! However helpful and pleasant Heba might be, there was no way Ashley wanted a maid in constant attendance. Orders be damned! She wouldn't stand for it no matter what the Sheikh said.

Ashley rose from the bed to do battle, but was distracted from her purpose by the arrival of her suitcases from the Sheraton Hotel. Heba immediately wanted to unpack them. The sight of those suitcases containing all the evidence of her presence in Egypt gave Ashley an even greater incentive for rebellion. To have them unpacked meant an acceptance that she would be staying here, and Ashley could not concede that. Not yet. Not ever, she thought with a grim ferocity that speared from her eyes as she turned on Heba.

'Don't you so much as touch those suitcases!' she cried vehemently. 'I want you out of this room, and you will stay out until I call for you.

Now go! Go! Or so help me God, I won't be answerable for the consequences.

The girl sprang to her feet with a cry of fear as Ashley advanced upon her. She did not wait to see what Ashley's intentions were, but ran for the door and scuttled out, hastily closing it behind her.

The violent upsurge of temper left Ashley feeling more exhausted, and she lay back down on the bed and closed her eyes, wishing for a sleep from which she would never waken; then wearily chided herself for the thought. Death was so terribly final. Even life with the Sheikh had to have some value. If she slept now, surely she could regain the strength to fight him again. Maybe he would leave her alone and not press his desire if she rejected him forcefully enough.

But what if he ignored her protests? If he simply swept words aside and took direct action ... kissed her and ... oh, God! She would surely get pregnant. It was the fertile period of her monthly cycle. If a child was conceived ... a baby ...

To have her very own child ... the old yearning swept through her, tugging at her heart, obliterating fear with a desire that was as old as time. If she stayed with him ... if he gave her a child ... a child ... Ashley clutched on to the thought. It gradually soothed away the turmoil, letting her drift into a peaceful, heavy sleep.

CHAPTER SIX

OUTSIDE the door of the Damascus Room, Heba waited until all sound of movement ceased, then nervously crept back into the room, gently tucked a mohair rug around her strange new mistress, and watched over her in deep concern for several hours.

Agitated by Ashley's stillness, the girl finally felt driven to report all that had happened to her master, whose dark frown did nothing to lighten her fear that she had done something terribly wrong. But when he finally noticed that she was hopping from foot to foot in sheer nervousness, he gave her a kindly smile.

'You have done well to tell me of this, Heba. For the present let her sleep on. It will be good for her. Later, I will come and see for myself.'

Heba flashed him a relieved smile, gave a low curtsy, and hurried back to her post beside Ashley's bed. When it became dark, she switched on one of the lamps so her new mistress would not be alarmed when she awoke. The light was dim and soft, too weak to disturb a sleeper.

Ashley was lifted into half-consciousness by the featherlight touch on her cheek. Her skin tingled from the caress, forcing an awareness through her mind. A more pervasive sensation brought her fully alert as fingers grazed over her jawline and down the long column of her neck to rest on her shoulder. Other fingertips brushed her temple, stroking tendrils of hair back from her face. Her heart leapt into a violent pumping action, and only an urgent command from her brain kept her from opening her eyes.

It was him. She didn't have to see to know it was only his touch that could stir this chaotic reaction. And she was so hopelessly vulnerable. Ashley willed herself to keep absolutely motionless, to pretend she was still asleep, so that he might go away and leave her alone. She wasn't ready to face him ... she needed time ... time to get herself under control.

The frantic necessity to keep her breathing even, to make the slow, regular inhalations of the sleeper, required the most intense concentration. If even one involuntary gasp escaped her, he would discover her ploy and take instant advantage of her apparent passivity.

His hand played soothingly over her brow, then so lightly over her eyes that Ashley was barely aware she had been touched. He brushed the hair away from her ear, his fingers straying delicately around the rim before he caressed the lobe. Exquisite sensation squirmed through her body, melting the defensive shield she had tried to create.

A hot flush of blood seeped through to the outermost layer of her skin; every hair on her body prickled with sensitivity. Surely he must be aware of what he was doing to her, aware that she could not be asleep. He was playing a silent, seductive cat-and-mouse game that she couldn't possibly win, but still she stubbornly clung to the pretence of sleep, postponing the inevitable, which was too frightening to face.

His hand dropped to her throat. Somehow Ashley controlled the desire to swallow, the desire to give up this hopeless charade. All he had to do was feel the artery throbbing in her neck with each pulsation of her heart to know that her body was responding to him with wanton eagerness.

For one wild moment Ashley wanted to believe that the way he was touching her could only be the product of loving tenderness; that it was not just lust, but a deep caring for all her needs. But reason forced her to discard that madness. It insisted that he only wanted to gratify his needs ... to own ... to dominate.

The hand on her shoulder slowly swept down towards her breast. Ashley could feel it poised, wanting to go further, yearning to touch her in a way only one other man ever had. If he did that to her when he thought she was asleep, she would pluck his eyes out. But the hand went no further, returning from where it had come.

Perhaps he knew she was awake and he was deliberately torturing her. The warmth of his breath fanned her cheek. It was a moment of acute terror. She knew what would come next. The effort to remain immobile made her hands go clammy. He was going to kiss her, and she did not know how she would get past the test.

Then she knew she didn't want to!

She could feel his presence so close to her that he

could only be millimetres away, and her mouth craved for the same erotic invasion of last night's kiss. The masculine scent of his body excited her, and through her mind ran a burst of exhilaration, tipping her inexorably towards surrender. She could feel her lips parting ever so slightly in blatant invitation. She was ashamed that she could participate so eagerly in her own seduction, in her own downfall, but did it really matter . . .? If there was a child . . .

The confusing tumult of thoughts was brushed away by the faintest touch of his lips against hers, tantalisingly sweet. She could not stop the shudder of pleasure that swept through her, the rampant need, the clawing expectation of more pressure that made her whole body ache for intimate contact; his weight and strength enveloping her, sinking into her, possessing her.

And then he was gone. She felt the mattress lift with his withdrawal, could not understand how this could be happening. Her body cried out in anguish for the promise of fulfilment.

Relief came like a crawling snail, leaving its path of shame as she recognised the narrowness of her escape. Perhaps he still believed that she was asleep. She didn't dare raise her eyelashes. She could feel his gaze on her, sense the desire he was repressing. It was so strong that every nerve in her body was still twitching in response.

He moved away, but he did not leave her. The soft fall of his footsteps told Ashley he was pacing up and down the huge rug near the window. He stopped at the far end, paused there for a long time, and the tension emanating from his presence drove Ashley to risk a covert peek at him.

He was dressed in white, but they were western clothes, the tailored trousers revealing a taut, masculine physique that exuded virility. The loose shirt of white silk was opened almost to the waist, giving her a glimpse of black curls sprinkling the darkly tanned skin. The sudden, urgent desire to touch him there, over the heartbeat she had felt this morning, was so strong that it shook Ashley to the very core of her being.

His head was bare and turned slightly towards the window. For the first time, Ashley was struck by the noble cast of his face. It was strong, commanding in its very strength. But it was not stamped with arrogance tonight. The interplay of expressions ranged from uncertainty to grim frustration.

That he should even feel hesitant about the course he had chosen astonished Ashley, but clearly he was in conflict. His gaze suddenly swung back to her and the black eyes were burning with pent-up need. He moved, and Ashley's heart pounded with alarm at the thought that, despite the dim light, he might have seen the tiny flicker of her eyelashes dropping shut.

He stood beside her for what seemed an eternity. She heard him sigh, then in an abrupt, decisive movement he left the room. Ashley could hardly believe it, even with the soft click of the door being shut behind him. She remained still for a long time, not daring to accept that he really meant to leave her alone.

Eventually she plucked up enough courage to open her eyes and look at her watch. It was almost ten o'clock. She had slept close to eight hours. Would he come back again when he was sure she could no longer be asleep? If so, Ashley could no longer delude herself that she would fight him. He only had to brush his lips against her own and she would give in to him.

She squirmed restlessly under the mohair blanket, all too appallingly aware of her susceptibility to his attraction and despising herself for it. She couldn't lie here like a sitting duck, waiting for him to fire a final arrow into her heart. And he would come back. She had seen the need eating into the incredible control he had maintained. It had to surface soon, sweeping aside every other consideration.

Ashley tossed the blanket aside and sprang to her feet, driven to take some course of defensive action. A visit to the bathroom was necessary, anyway. Her skirt and tunic were crumpled, but she dismissed the impulse to open her suitcases and change into fresh clothes. It might be a petty and futile act of defiance, but at least it would show him that she was not resigned to staying in this damned house!

She splashed water on her face and regretted that she couldn't brush her hair. The mirrored walls of the bathroom did nothing for her morale, so she made a quick exit. A shudder of apprehension ran through her as she contemplated a return to the Damascus Room. She took the opposite direction, hurrying along the corridor, frantically thinking there must be some place she could hide, some place where she couldn't be immediately found.

However stupid the idea was, Ashley did not have any others to act on, so she pushed on, discarding one room after another until she reached the 'harim'. Did the Sheikh know of the secret room?

Of course he would, Ashley berated herself. But he might not know that she had been shown it. Driven by the need to keep away from him as long as possible, to hide herself from him, Ashley opened the cupboard door and stepped into the tiny gallery.

The voice from the *qa'ah* below almost caused her to trip over a stool. The hard, distinctive tone of it rang in her ears like some inescapable echo. But then another voice spoke and hope leapt in her heart. It hardly seemed possible. How could it be so? She crept to the screen and looked down. She had not been mistaken. it was him! Louis-Philippe! The Baron de Laclos. And he was facing the Sheikh with an imperturbable air of authority.

Amazement quickly melted into relief. All she had to do was cry out to him, begging his help. No matter what Azir said, she was sure Louis-Philippe would take her side. He knew enough about her to realise that she would not spin such an outrageous story. But as she drew breath, he spoke, and the words were so shocking, the tone so chilling, that Ashley froze into horrified silence.

'The war in Algeria taught many of us the more barbaric methods of interrogation. Few men can remain loyally silent when a knife is biting into their naked flesh. So don't blame your chauffeur! He had to tell the truth. So I know you had Ashley Cunningham abducted. I know she is here.'

The silence that followed simmered with antagonism. Ashley held her breath. She was watching some deadly conflict, a contest of wills that diminished her own plight. The two men stood some considerable distance apart, as tense as two gladiators in the ring, assessing each other, waiting ... waiting like coiled springs for a glimmer of vulnerability before rejoining battle.

'The Algerian war taught many lessons,' Azir finally answered, his tone laced with bitter contempt. 'How to kill helpless women and children ...'

The Baron de Laclos did not flinch. The accusation made no impression on him whatsoever. His face remained completely impassive, his gaze steadily fixed on the blazing black eyes of Azir Talil Khaybar.

'You know I did my utmost to prevent the massacre of innocent lives. You know I was court-martialled for disobeying those orders. Blame your father for using the villagers and putting their lives in jeopardy ...'

'They were prepared to lay down their lives to get the French out of their country,' came the fierce retort. 'What right did you have to subjugate the Arab people and take their land?'

'We could argue that question all night. We've already fought a war over it. It achieves nothing. I've long since lost all interest in politics. Whatever you think of my . . . participation . . . I paid for it. And I paid for your father's freedom. You know he owes his life to me. That's what I've come for. I'm calling in the debt.'

Ashley had recognised the ruthlessness in Azir Talil Khaybar at first sight, but she had not even sensed it in Louis-Philippe de Laclos. She stared down at him, trying to match the gentle man she had met last night to the man she saw now. A deadly determination was graven on his face, and the sad, grey eyes were unrelenting steel.

'No!' The word exploded from Azir's throat, harsh and violent.

Louis-Philippe's mouth thinned in contempt. 'A man of honour would not deny me.'

'Ask for any other of my possessions and you can have it. Our family pays its debts,' Azir retorted with cold, stinging pride. 'Take whatever you want, Frenchman.'

'A life for a life, Azir,' came the relentless demand. 'Have the girl brought to me. That's all I ask.'

'We no longer keep slaves,' Azir replied, his voice dropping to a low rasp. 'She is not mine to give.'

'Nor yours to take,' Louis retorted sharply. 'You had her abducted, Azir, and she wasn't a willing victim. It was you she ran from last night, you who put the fear in her eyes . . .'

'And me she wants!' The words hung in the air between them, vibrating with suppressed emotion.

'Then let her tell me that,' was the quiet, but

equally lethal reply.

It was a simple matter for her to call out, to end the confrontation being enacted below her, but Ashley still hesitated. The elemental clash of character, the raw revelation of feelings that throbbed beneath the surface of their masks, held her spellbound. Was Azir's desire for her so strong that he valued her above all his other possessions? She waited, her heart pounding in her ears as she strained to hear his reply.

'She is asleep,' he said in a low, dismissive tone. 'And I will not have her disturbed.'

'Take me to her!'

'No! Come back tomorrow.'

The concession astonished Ashley until she realised how many hours there were before tomorrow. Was he gambling that he could tie her to him with his lovemaking? Or was he playing for time to remove her from Louis-Philippe's reach?

The grey eyes narrowed. 'I will not leave this house without her, Azir.' The flat, unequivocal statement held relentless purpose.

'Then either you will have to kill me . . . or I will have to kill you.'

The low, vibrant words echoed and re-echoed through Ashley's mind, but still she couldn't believe that they had been spoken. It was not until Azir strode down the room and drew the sword of Salah al-Din from its scabbard that the reality was stamped home. The scream that tore from Ashley's throat reverberated around the huge two-storeyed room.

'No-o-o! No-o-o!' She beat at the *mashra-*

biyyah screen with frenzied hands.

'Ashley!'

She saw Louis-Philippe's face turn up to her, but her frantic gaze sought Azir's.

'Stop it! You can't do this!' she cried, in desperate fear of the ruthless will behind the sword.

He lifted a grim face to the gallery where she stood shaking with terror. His eyes burned with fierce command. 'Then tell him you will stay with me. Tell him now, Ashley, and send him away.'

'No!' Louis-Philippe barked the counter-command. He strode down the room to where Azir held his position and came to a halt with barely a yard between them. 'You won't get her by force, Azir. We both know that if you kill me, you'll lose, anyway. My death will hang like an albatross around your neck, and she'll never look at you without seeing it.'

'Oh, God!' Ashley sobbed, and forced her voice to a scream. 'Please stop it! Both of you!' Again she beat on the screen in helpless frustration, too terrified to move in case something happened while she tried to find her way down to them.

Light flashed from the sword. It wavered in Azir's hand. She saw the tortured heave of his chest under the white silk of his shirt. His head suddenly jerked up, his gaze probing the screen behind which she stood, and the conflict that raged within him was written on his face. Pain, such as she had never thought to see in him, flowed up at her, wound around her heart, pleading, demanding recognition.

'Ashley!' It was a hoarse, driven cry. 'Say it! Say you want to stay with me!'

'I can't,' she sobbed, torn beyond bearing. 'Don't do it, Azir. Please . . .'

She could not look at his face any longer. Her gaze dropped to the sword in his hand. She saw the clenched grip tighten, saw the blade swing as if to strike, felt horror strangling her throat. Then the sword was arcing through the air, clattering on to the marble floor, tipping into the fountain. And all the breath in her body was released in a tortured sigh.

Some automatic process set her feet moving. Shock still glazed her mind, but her legs pounded along the corridors, down the flight of steps, through the passageway that led to the qa'ah. She burst open the door at the back of the room, ran on past the fountain and threw herself against Louis-Philippe de Laclos, sobbing with relief that he had not been injured. A strong arm came around her, hugging her tight. A hand gently stroked her hair. 'It's all right, Ashley. We can go now. It's over.'

The soft murmur ravaged her heart. It was over. She was free, yet every instinct screamed that she would never be free of this day . . . this night. A terrible uncertainty ripped through her mind.

A harsh, soft laughter echoed through the qa'ah. 'It's not over. It will never be over. But my father's life is now repaid, Frenchman. From here our paths go separate ways.'

The dull finality in Azir's voice hurt Ashley in some indefinable way. She turned, pulled by a need that she didn't stop to question. But the pained black eyes passed over her without recognition, and the harsh, arrogant face was carved in stone.

'Go! You have chosen,' he said in a flat monotone. 'May you find your happiness.'

This last was a bare whisper as he set off, leading the way to the double entrance doors. Louis-Philippe dropped his arm around Ashley's waist, half-supporting her as he pushed her into walking the length of the room. Azir opened the doors, barked orders in Arabic, then stood back for them to pass.

Ashley was intensely, frighteningly aware of his taut body, so rigidly motionless as Louis-Philippe steered her to the top of the steps which led down to the courtyard. Her feet faltered, stopped, turned, drawn by a power beyond her control.

The hurt was so bad, she had to try and explain. 'It wouldn't have worked, Azir,' she said softly.

He looked at her then, the black eyes seeing straight into her soul.

'You should have listened to your heart, Ashley. I did.' And with that bleak utterance he turned and walked back up the room to the fountain. Just before the doors swung shut, Ashley saw him stoop to retrieve the sword of Salah al-Din.

She shivered, remembering the way he had pressed into the tip of the blade this morning . . . so sure of himself, so sure of her. A hand grasped her elbow and she dragged her gaze up to the sad, blue-grey eyes that had softened in concern for her.

'Ashley, we must go now. He is strained to the limits of control.'

'Yes. Yes, of course,' she murmured distractedly.

Louis-Philippe took her at her word, steering her away and lending his strength to her tottering footsteps. No one stopped them. Even when they stepped outside, down the steps to the cobbled cul-de-sac, the guards there stood respectfully aside and waved them on to the gateway.

She stubbed her toes on the rough roadway and loked down at them dazedly, having forgotten that her feet were bare. Her sandals were still lying beside the bed in the Damascus Room. And not only her sandals! She stopped dead, the churning sense of loss deepening into panic. She plucked wildly at Louis-Philippe's arm.

'We've got to go back. All my things are here ... money, passport, my folder, everything ...'

He shook his head. 'You can't go back! He would never let you go again. You saw what it cost to buy your freedom this time!'

He was right. She knew he was right. But a wild hysteria clawed up her throat and spilled off her tongue. 'You don't understand! I haven't got anything! All the sketches I've done ... my airline tickets ... my passport ... how do I even get out of the country?'

Louis-Philippe's arm tightened around her. 'They can all be replaced. I will look after you. Whatever you need can be bought tomorrow.'

Again he carried her along with him, sweeping her out to the narrow, unlit street where a car stood waiting in the darkness. He bundled Ashley into the back seat, followed her in, slammed the door and threw a curt command at the driver. The car accelerated away, and only then did Ashley realise that tears were trickling down her cheeks.

She couldn't stop them. There were too many emotions welling inside her, needing some release. And the ache in her heart ... why did it ache so?

CHAPTER SEVEN

AN arm curled around Ashley, and Louis-Philippe gently tucked her head on to his shoulder. He pressed a clean handkerchief into her hand. 'We'll soon be back at the hotel,' he murmured.

Ashley tried to mop up the tears but her eyes kept overflowing. 'I ... I haven't even thanked you. It was so much. So ...'

'It was only a matter of knowing how to proceed,' he said dismissively. 'Once I knew it was Azir ...'

He did not finish his thought, and Ashley could not find the will to pursue the matter further. The traumatic scene with Azir was still too close, too raw, too laden with pain. She sensed that Louis-Philippe didn't want to talk about it, and neither did she.

'It will never be over.' Azir's words hammered through her heart. But what else could she have done? Azir had demanded an impossible choice from her ... hadn't he? How could she have stayed? Louis-Philippe had risked his very life to rescue her, and she had been frantic to escape Azir. There had been no other choice. None. She shivered at the memory of his touch on her skin... the look in his eyes ...

'You're suffering from shock,' Louis-Philippe

murmured, hugging her more closely to him for warmth. 'We're almost at the hotel.'

Indeed, within a few moments the car was slowing to a halt at the front entrance of the Sheraton. Louis-Philippe helped her out, then whisked her up the steps and through the lobby where people were still milling around the shops and food-bars.

'Ashley! Ashley!'

Sohaila's beautiful young voice floated through the reception area, totally distinctive in its accent. Ashley's head jerked up in time to see her friend come flying across the room, her black curls bobbing, her lovely face lit with excitement. She threw her arms around Ashley and hugged her close.

'You're safe! You're safe! Oh, Ashley, I was so worried for you. When the Baron found out what had happened, I thought I would never see you again.'

The Baron ... and Sohaila ... and Ahmed, Sohaila's fiancé, looming up behind her ... Ashley didn't understand any of it, but she was relieved to see her friend, to feel her life moving back on to familiar rails.

Sohaila drew back, falling naturally into the mannerisms that Ashley found so endearing. Her whole body moved as she spoke, an expressive lift of her shoulders or wriggle of her hips; the delicate gestures of her fingers and hands; the lovely almond eyes flashing white as she rolled her irises.

'I did not know what to do when you didn't come to the museum, so I came here and asked for you and they said you'd checked out, which I felt couldn't be right. And then I saw the Baron and he . . .' Her eyes flashed to the man behind Ashley, and they shone with admiration. 'He found out where you were.'

As if recollecting herself, her gaze returned anxiously to Ashley. 'There was nothing I could do, you understand. The Sheikh . . . his power and prestige . . . not even MISR could act against him without the President's authority.'

The flat statement of fact shook Ashley. Despite Azir's claim of diplomatic immunity, she had not realised that only the President of Egypt would dare move against him. Yet Louis-Philippe de Laclos had done precisely that!

Her gaze lifted wonderingly to the enigmatic man who had so many hidden depths. Even now his face was shuttered, slightly stiff as if he had once more donned a mask, retreating behind it to the weariness of soul that had been so eloquently expressed last night.

'Sohaila, you have seen that your friend is safe now,' Ahmed stated pointedly. The finely drawn cast of his handsome features emanated disapproval, and it was plain that he did not like his fiancée's attachment to these foreigners.

A deep flush burned over Sohaila's beautiful olive skin. 'Ahmed, Ashley needs my help,' she pleaded.

He took in Ashley's dishevelled hair, the

pinched paleness of her face, the crumpled clothes and bare feet, then shot a cynically knowing look at the Frenchman.

'Perhaps you can help Ashley tomorrow, Sohaila,' Louis suggested quietly. 'You can safely leave her in my care tonight.'

'Yes. Yes, of course. I'm sorry, I ...' She faltered and turned pained eyes to Ashley. 'I'll come in the morning.'

Ashley squeezed her hand. 'Thank you for all you've done. For caring enough to ...'

'Oh, Ashley!' Tears blurred the luminous, dark eyes and once again Sohaila hugged her close. 'I'm happy you are safe,' she whispered huskily.

Her friend's affection moved Ashley deeply. The abduction today had probably cast her in the role of a fallen woman by Moslem standards. Condemnation was written on Ahmed's face as he stood sullenly beside them.

Ashley quickly disentangled herself from Sohaila's embrace and flicked an appeasing look at her friend's stern fiancé. 'It was good of you both to wait. I appreciate it very deeply.'

Ahmed took Sohaila's arm and said a curt goodbye for both of them. As the two Egyptians walked away, the hand on Ashley's elbow tightened its grip to a painful clench and she looked up at Louis-Philippe in mute protest. His face wore a grim tightness and she caught a glimpse of some intense emotion in his eyes before he glanced down at her.

'I'm sorry. I find it difficult to tolerate such rudeness.'

'He was probably tired ...'

Louis-Philippe relaxed and lifted his arm to curl comfortingly around Ashley's shoulders. An ironic smile softened his mouth as he added, 'Perhaps you're right. The tyranny of culture creates a chasm we cannot cross.'

An elevator opened its doors behind them, and Louis-Philippe steered her into it. Ashley felt discomfited by the awkward parting from Sohaila and Ahmed, but it was only a tiny addition to the depression that weighed on her heart.

Louis-Philippe had summed the truth up in a few words. It couldn't have worked with Azir, no matter how deep the attraction. The culture difference was too daunting. She leaned tiredly against Louis-Philippe, intensely grateful for his support and understanding, and when the elevator reached his floor, she accompanied him to his suite without the slightest hesitation. The sense of kinship she had felt with him last night was even stronger now.

They didn't talk much, both of them preoccupied with their own thoughts, and both of them automatically respecting the other's silences. Louis-Philippe ordered a meal which neither of them showed much interest in. He organised a room for her on the same floor as his corner suite, just along the corridor so that she could easily call on him if she felt nervous about anything. He had given his word to Sohaila that he would take care of her, and he did.

'Why?' Ashley asked at one point. 'You hardly know me, Louis.'

He gave his sad, ironic smile. 'Perhaps an old-fashioned sense of chivalry. Sohaila asked me to help her. You asked me to help you last night. And the war in Algeria left its scars.' He paused and shot her a sharp, probing look. 'But Azir didn't act without reason, did he, Ashley?'

'He had reason,' she admitted. 'But he had no right to take me like that. And I could not have been happy with that kind of life.'

'Yes. That is always the bottom line. And force can't get you what you want. Not what you really want,' Louis-Philippe murmured. He sighed and startled Ashley by adding, 'Still, I can sympathise with Azir.'

She looked askance at him, remembering the ruthlessness he had displayed tonight and wondering what he really wanted.

He shrugged. 'How much longer do you need to be in Egypt, Ashley?'

'Only a week or two if I could get a favourable decision out of the government.'

'Perhaps I can help you. I have some little influence that might ease the way. If you like, I shall talk to some people tomorrow and ...' He paused as he saw her puzzlement. 'It is better finished, is it not? For you to go home and forget this?'

'Yes. Yes, I suppose it is,' she agreed. She had been too long in this foreign country. She was even causing trouble between Sohaila and Ahmed, not helping her friend at all. 'Thank you, Louis. I would be grateful for any help I can get from anyone.'

He nodded. 'I'll let you know. Would dinner tomorrow night be convenient?'

'Yes. Thank you.'

'It is sometimes . . . invigorating . . . to be of use.'

Their eyes met in understanding and there was nothing more to say. Louis-Philippe saw Ashley into her new room and they parted sympathetic friends.

Ashley was woken by a porter's call the next morning. Azir had returned everything to her; the two suitcases, her handbag containing her passport, money and airline tickets, and the sketch folder that represented so many weeks of hard work. There was no accompanying note. No message.

Ashley told herself she should feel relieved. Azir had accepted her choice. She would never see him again; it was finished. But no relief came. The aching sense of loss she had felt at parting with Azir intensified, raising tormenting questions in her mind.

Would she have been unhappy with him? He had reached into her, touching depths she had never recognised in herself before, awakening desires to a more vibrant life than she had ever known. She had craved for his touch, craved to feel . . . everything!

Madness, she told herself once again, but it did

not take the ache away, and Ashley felt thoroughly miserable as she unpacked her suitcases and changed into fresh clothes. She forced herself to eat breakfast in the wan hope that food might fill the void, but it didn't.

She put a call through to Louis-Philippe's room and informed him that all her belongings had been returned. 'So I can get straight on with my work,' she concluded, and thanked him once again for the support he had offered.

Louis-Philippe had certainly given her the right advice—wrap up her business in Egypt as quickly as possible and get back home, away from all things foreign. She was going mad here! The idea of gambling her money away should have been warning enough.

By the time Sohaila arrived, Ashley was ready to go to the museum and get on with her work. The Egyptian girl was clearly relieved that everything had apparently returned to normal.

'Are you sure you're all right, Ashley?' she asked anxiously.

'Of course,' Ashley assured her with a smile.

An embarrassed flush crept into Sohaila's cheeks. 'I am sorry that I had to leave last night. I did not think . . . like Ahmed . . .' She floundered, her hands gesturing an anxious apology.

'I understand, Sohaila,' Ashley said in soft sympathy. 'I hope I didn't cause you any trouble with your fiancé.'

Sohaila shrugged and her mouth tightened into a stubborn line. 'It does not matter. I can think for myself, can I not?'

'Well, I'm certainly glad you did yesterday,' Ashley said lightly, wanting to dispel the slight awkwardness of the moment. 'If you hadn't spoken to Louis I would have been in terrible trouble. I'm immensely grateful to you, Sohaila.'

The colour in Sohaila's cheeks ebbed and flowed. 'He is a wonderful man ... the Baron. So kind.'

'He certainly is,' Ashley agreed warmly. 'He's even offered to help me get the permission needed for the jewellery exhibition. Isn't that marvellous?'

'Yes,' Sohaila agreed, but her enthusiasm was shadowed by some other, indefinable emotion.

'What's the problem, Sohaila?' Ashley asked bluntly. 'You're not yourself at all.'

The expressive mouth turned down into a self-mocking grimace. 'I was thinking you will be leaving our country soon, Ashley. And I will miss you.'

'I'll miss you, too,' Ashley sighed, then linked her arm with her friend's and forced a cheer-up smile. 'But I'm not gone yet, so let's enjoy today.'

Once at the museum, they went straight to the north wing which housed the Tutankhamun galleries. Nearby was the Jewel Room which contained the pharaonic artefacts from many dynasties, and it was here that Ashley had seen the bracelets she wanted to sketch. Sohaila found them both chairs and they settled down to work beside the showcases.

The cylindrical bracelets had the most immediate eye-impact with their designs of winged scarabs and sun-disks and the cartouches of the kings; all gold inlaid with lapis lazuli, cornelian and green felspar. Ashley did not doubt their selling-power, but she was fairly certain that the daintier type of hoop bracelet which had been found on the mummy of the high-priest Pinudjem would have even more buyer appeal.

The last seemed to be the forerunner of today's charm bracelet. From two small rings near the clasp fell a number of tassels, some ending in lapis lazuli pendants in the form of hexagonal pyramids; others were strung with beads which supported gold flowerettes formed by six conjoined petals. The workmanship in the flowerettes was exquisite, and Ashley marvelled over it as she sketched.

Sohaila's incredibly detailed knowledge of the relics of Ancient Egypt allowed her to tell Ashley the meaning of every design in the jewellery. Invariably, she added entertaining stories about the people who had worn the pieces. When Ashley thought some detail was particularly relevant, she would get Sohaila to write it out. In this way each piece acquired its own fascinating history.

Time passed all too quickly. Ashley skipped lunch, but sent Sohaila off to have something to eat in the museum cafeteria. Her friend had been gone some ten minutes when Ashley felt the man's presence. Even as she berated herself for the wildness of her imagination—it could not be him, it was all over, he would never see her again—her gaze was drawn from her sketch-pad and pulled towards the archway at the other end of the gallery.

Azir stood there. He was clothed as she had first seen him, as formidable now as he had been then, and Ashley's reaction was instant and over-whelming. Her mind crackled with hot, frantic explosions of thought. A quiver of electric excitement ran through her body; catching her breath, cramping her heart, and digging a queezy hollowness in her stomach.

He stepped forward, the dark eyes devouring her in a way that was a violation in itself. Ashley forced herself to stand. The folder slipped from her nerveless hands, spilling the contents over the floor. The light sound of her pencil hitting the stonework seemed to reverberate throughout the room.

'You must not be frightened of me, Ashley. You have nothing to fear. You never did. Although I understand why you do not see it that way.' His voice was quiet, the tone tense.

Her hand instinctively crept to cover her heart, which had burst from its constriction and was pounding its wild agitation against the wall of her chest. 'Why ...' The word was a graceless croak. She swallowed convulsively and tried again. 'Why are you here? I thought ... when you sent back my bags ... I never expected to see you again.'

The muscles in his face tightened; his eyes darkened with a ravening hunger that tore at her own feeble composure. 'I could not live with myself if I did not try to make some reparation for the wrongs I have done you ... for the terrible mistake in judgement that I made ... and for the pain I gave you.'

Reparation! The word shattered the wanton hope that had fluttered through Ashley's mind. 'Oh, please ...' she begged, swamped by a wave of intense humiliation. She had to send him away before he realised his power over her. Sheer despair lent strength to her voice. 'There's no need to say or do anything. I don't want ...'

'Will you not hear me out, Ashley?' he interrupted softly.

The request tugged at her heart, and she could not refuse him, no matter how hard it was to keep some grain of self-possession in his presence.

He paused only a moment or two, then continued with a quiet deliberation that projected a strong emotional impact into every word. 'I had no right to take anything from you. Not your possessions ... nor your freedom. My blind desire to keep you with me overruled every other consideration. Even humanity.'

His mouth twisted into a bitter grimace of self-contempt. 'I deluded myself! Even when I knew ... Heba told me how distressed you were ... I still clung on to the belief that ... I had to be right.'

'And ... and now?' Ashley asked, driven by her own need for a solution that would allow her to meet him in some acceptable way.

'And now ... I accept the consequences ... and

I hope . . . make some recompense for the pain I caused you.'

He walked towards her and every nerve in Ashley's body twanged with an expectation that was impossible to control. She couldn't move. Her legs almost gave way when he stooped at her feet. But it was not to touch her.

For the first time she noticed he carried a parcel, carelessly wrapped in brown paper, and fastened with twine. He threw it aside on the chair she had vacated, then turned his attention to the sheets of sketches that had scattered on the floor. He retrieved them all with meticulous care, replacing them one by one in her folder. With the task completed, he lifted the parcel and slid the portfolio under it.

When he straightened up he was barely an arm's distance away, and Ashley felt she was being sucked into the dark whirlpools of passion that were his eyes. His voice fell softly, yet struck chords of recognition that quivered in response.

'You called it lust, Ashley. Perhaps it is, but I don't believe it. Never before in my life have I ever experienced such an instant, compelling attraction for a woman. When I first saw you, it was as if my whole being leapt in excitement. And with every second that passed, I grew more certain that my life could never be complete without you. I can control lust. I could not control what I felt for you.'

His hand reached over and took hers, reinforcing his words with a gentle stroking that was more compelling than any possessive grip.

'You will never comprehend the violence of my rage when I believed you had forsaken me to sleep with the Baron de Laclos. The thought that under the beauty of your face and body lay the wantonness of a whore ...'

'No!' Her own anguish of spirit forced the denial. She was not a whore, and yet with Azir ...

His other hand lifted to stroke her cheek in tender apology. 'You think I don't know that now? That I am not deeply shamed by what you told me?'

It was madness, utter madness, but the urge to nestle her cheek into the warm palm of his hand was so primal she almost gave way to it. Her skin heated and quivered under the light touch, and the despairing appeal in his eyes tore at her heart.

'I was deranged by what seemed to be irrefutable evidence that you were not the woman I wanted you to be. I despised myself for still wanting you, yet I could not rid myself of the need to have you with me. And then I found I was wrong. That I had deceived myself. And you made it ... abundantly clear that I had destroyed any chance I had of your staying with me of your own free will.'

The lingering finger-touch trailed from her cheek, his hand dropping reluctantly to his side. 'Not only that,' he added bitterly, 'but I'd condemned myself so much in your eyes that I had no hope of your agreeing to see me again if I let you go.'

The memory of his cold callousness as he ordered her imprisonment stung Ashley into a reply. 'You didn't give me that choice, Azir.'

His eyes mocked her. 'Ashley, there was only one course left to take and I took it. You couldn't think any worse of me, and I hoped, in time, I could persuade you that ...' He stopped, and his expression hardened. 'Given the same circumstances I would make the same decision again. The miscalculation was in overestimating your ... reaction to me, and in underestimating your attachment to the Baron de Laclos.'

That shook Ashley out of the draining weakness which had almost betrayed her. Azir's remorse might be genuine, but there was no ignoring the intrinsic ruthlessness in his character. It would lead to utter self-abasement if she gave in to him. He had left her in no doubt that he wanted to own her body and soul. Did she really want a relationship that demanded so much of her that she was left with no identity of her own?

'I must make my own decisions, Azir,' she said defensively, frightened by his power over her, and all too aware of his ability to sweep aside all the normal safeguards of the law. 'I won't have that right taken away from me.'

Something dangerous glittered in his eyes. His fingers closed more firmly around her hand, re-asserting the physical link between them. 'The decision you made last night . . . was it the right one, Ashley?'

Confusion swirled through her mind. His thumb caressed her wrist and it was impossible to concentrate on anything else. Her whole body was prickling with sensual awareness, aching for the resolution only he could give her.

Had she made the right decision? There was no other she could have made at the time, and yet . . . the tumult of emotions he aroused in her . . . the intensive desire he could evoke just by looking at her . . . if she confessed what she felt, he would sweep her away. And then . . . could she live his life? Be content as his mistress?

'Ashley . . . answer me!'

The urgent pressure of his voice . . . his hand . . . his eyes probing into her . . . taking her over . . . leaving her no other existence except as his possession.

'Yes! Yes, I made the right decision,' she cried, almost panting from the effort needed to deny him.

And another, different cry trembled on her tongue as his eyes dulled and he released her hand. Every instinct clamoured to recapture his attention, his touch, uncaring of the consequences. He turned and started to walk away, and the clamour of her mind increased, drowning out the voice of reason.

'Azir!'

He stopped abruptly, then half turned, his face totally expressionless. Ashley's mind went into a spin, frantically reaching for a way that could make their relationship work.

'It was partly my fault . . . the way I acted at the casino. I don't blame you for . . . for thinking the worst of me.'

There was no reaction from him. He simply waited patiently for her to continue, his dark gaze fixed unblinkingly on hers, hard and unreadable. Ashley groped for a resolution that would allow her time to consider what a future with Azir might mean to her.

'I . . . I don't think badly of you. Now that we understand each other better, couldn't we meet . . . as friends?'

'No, Ashley.' There was a wafting quality of sadness in his voice. 'We can never be friends. You and I can only be lovers!'

The temptation to give in and fling herself at him was almost irresistible. The prospect of being totally immersed with him held its own compelling fascination, but Ashley could not quite set aside the practical reality that to love this man would necessitate her throwing off attitudes and beliefs she had held all her life.

Slowly she shook her head in negation.

'I could not be content with anything less,' he said softly. 'Between us, it has to be all or nothing.' And with that flat ultimatum, he turned away and walked on towards the archway through which he had entered the room.

Ashley searched her mind for anything to keep him with her longer, to prevent this final retreat

away from her. There was nothing. Her gaze
darted abstractedly over the display cases ... the
jewellery that had seemed so important to her ...
just meaningless objects. Her folder of designs ...
the parcel!

'Azir!' She snatched it up as if it was a lifeline.
'You've forgotten your parcel!'

He paused for just the briefest moment, flung
the words over his shoulder at her. 'No! That is
yours. I hope it gives you the joy you expected of
it.' And then he was gone.

Ashley sank down on Sohaila's chair, too bereft
to organise any rational thought. A deathlike
drum kept hammering on her heart. Azir had gone
... gone ... and gone with him was the last chance
of their becoming lovers ... the last chance of
knowing, of experiencing what it might have been
like if she'd had the courage to grasp all ... instead
of nothing.

Sohaila's hands gripped her shoulders tightly,
her lovely almond eyes dilating in alarm. 'Ashley!
Ashley! Are you all right?'

'Yes, of course,' Ashley replied automatically.
'Why wouldn't I be?'

'The Sheikh's guards blocked off the room.
They would not let me enter. I feared ...' Her
arms went round Ashley's shoulders, hugging her
in comfort and relief.

'It's all right. I'm fine. Truly.' The words
tripped out; stupid, empty words.

Sohaila anxiously searched her eyes. 'He didn't
hurt you?'

'No. He never meant to,' Ashley answered dully. But she had just hurt him, and herself, and that truth could not be dismisssed so easily. She sucked in a deep breath and forced a smile to relieve Sohaila's mind. 'He just wanted to say he was sorry for yesterday, and to give me this.' She picked up the parcel from the chair and was surprised to find it was quite heavy.

'What is it?' Sohaila asked, unable to restrain her curiosity.

'I don't know. Azir said it was mine. Something that was left behind, I guess.'

More for the sake of something to do than out of curiosity she began to unwrap the parcel in a half-hearted and desultory fashion. She frowned over the protective layers of tissue papers, and with a spurt of impatience tore them aside. The sheer magnificence of the gift left her gaping in astonishment. Because it was a gift. Ashley had never owned anything like it before in her life.

The jewellery-box was similar to that found among the treasures in Tutankhamun's tomb; exquisitely carved wood, inlaid with turquoise and gold. It had to be incredibly expensive, and Ashley wondered if this was what Azir meant when he spoke of making reparation for the pain he had caused her. She unfastened the catch and lifted the lid.

The neat stacks of American currency stared back at her. They were all one hundred dollar bills. Ashley did not have to count it. She knew exactly how much would be there. Ten thousand dollars.

The amount she had wanted to win at the roulette table in the casino. And Azir's last words to her echoed through her mind—'I hope it gives you the joy you expected of it'.

Sohaila's gasp of astonishment hardly impinged on her consciousness. Ashley's heart was a lump of cold stone. Azir was paying her off, making complete restitution for whatever he had done to her, expiating his mistake of judgement, driving the final nail into her coffin of need.

'He must love you very much!'

Sohaila's quiet words astonished Ashley. She looked at the girl for the first time since she unwrapped the parcel. The dark irises were rolled back in her head with amazement, her hands still thrown up in the air in surprise. The fingers gesticulated in emphasis as she repeated. 'He must love you. To give you such a present ...' The words trailed away as she searched for adequate words to express what she felt.

Ashley patted her friend's arm with a mixture of affection and sadness. 'No, Sohaila,' she said, and each word was a stab of pain as she dragged out the truth. 'It's not so. Azir doesn't love me. This isn't even a present for me. He knows I don't want the money. It's for you.'

CHAPTER EIGHT

SOHAILA stared at the money, then back at Ashley, her eyes widening in shocked denial. She shook her head vehemently. 'No, Ashley! How can it be so? The money has to be for you. The Sheikh does not even know me.'

Ashley ignored her. She hastily rewrapped the box and rose to her feet in a burst of purposeful energy. 'We can't talk about it here. Come back to the hotel with me and I'll explain.'

Sohaila was full of puzzled protests, but Ashley determinedly steered her out of the museum and into a taxi. There might not be any joy in it for her right at this moment, but Ashley felt a bitter satisfaction in knowing that someone was going to get some happiness out of all this mess, and that someone was going to be Sohaila.

At least her friend could have the future she wanted. As for her own future ... that was a bigger, darker question mark than it had ever been, and she couldn't bear to contemplate it. Ashley was intensely grateful that she had one action in hand that could be counted as a positive achievement.

Once inside her hotel room, with privacy ensured, Ashley re-opened the box and tipped its contents on to the bed. 'It's all yours, Sohaila! Ten thousand American dollars! And it was won at the roulette table in the casino downstairs. That's where I met the Sheikh.'

'You were gambling?' Sohaila gasped, still hopelessly bewildered.

'All in a good cause,' Ashley retorted firmly. 'And that cause was to win enough money so that you and Ahmed won't have to wait any longer to get your apartment. You can get married now, Sohaila! There'll be no in-laws breathing over your shoulder. No economic problems. You can start your marriage free and clear. It's all yours.'

Shock and pain drained the colour from Sohaila's face. She backed away, putting out a trembling hand as if to ward off the gift. 'No,' she whispered in a strained, hoarse voice. 'It's all wrong. I cannot take it.'

Ashley had expected some confusion from Sohaila initially; eventually delight and happiness at what the gift entailed. She had certainly never anticipated the horror in her reaction. It could only be due to the large sum of money involved.

'I want you to have it.' Ashley insisted firmly, anxious to put her friend at ease, and resolve the matter before Sohaila's negative attitude locked her into a position from which she could not retreat with dignity. 'I only went to the casino to help you. I have no need of the money. Azir helped me win it. Even he knew that it was to help a friend, not for me. I want you and Ahmed to be happy.'

Tears welled into the lovely dark eyes and Sohaila shook her head in hopeless distress. 'I cannot . . . I cannot marry Ahmed.'

'What?'

The tactless squawk made Sohaila turn away. She burst into heart-rending sobs. Clearly there was something terribly wrong, and it wasn't the money. Ashley gently drew the girl into her arms and tried to soothe her convulsive weeping.

'Why? After all these years of waiting?'

The words when they came were so incoherent that it took Ashley some time to understand them. 'I ... don't ... love ... him.'

She suddenly recalled Sohaila's strained manner this morning. And Ahmed's sullen air of disapproval last night. Had they argued about Sohaila's friendship with her? Was she the unwitting cause of this wretched misery? The thought worried Ashley so much that she had to speak.

'Sohaila, have I caused any trouble between you and Ahmed?'

'No ... I am sorry ... for losing control. I just ... cannot help myself, Ashley,' came the halting reply.

'Come and sit down on the bed and when you're ready, we'll talk about it. Maybe I can help.'

'No ...' Sohaila sobbed despairingly, but she sank on to the bed at Ashley's urging and tried to mop up the tears with the tissues handed to her.

'Sohaila, you must tell me. There can't be anything so terribly wrong that it can't be fixed up.'

A paroxysm of grief shook the girl, and she cried uncontrollably as Ashley put her arms around her in comfort and concern. As best she could, Ashley tried to soothe her, letting Sohaila cry out the tormented passion that drove her to such despair. Gradually the racking sobs quieted, and she drew away from Ashley's embrace, hunching over in self-conscious shame.

Ashley took her hand and squeezed it in affectionate encouragement. 'Sometimes it's good to cry, Sohaila. It releases all the pent-up feelings that we can't carry around any longer. And talking about them can help, too. Don't feel shy with me. Aren't I your friend?'

She nodded, then slowly lifted her tear-stained face. Her inner anguish still shimmered in the reddened eyes as she struggled to explain. 'I tried ... I tried to break off our engagement twice, Ashley. Once when I was seventeen—and again just before I graduated from the University. Both times my family put such pressure on me ... the shame ... the disgrace ... the humiliation. If I didn't honour the contract with Ahmed, no one else would want me anyway. My parents made my life such a misery ...'

She sucked in a deep breath and let it out on a shuddering sigh. 'I thought about leaving the country ... leaving everything. But you see ... I would not belong anywhere else. In the end, I decided I would do my best to make Ahmed a good wife. But I put it off as long as possible. That is why I insisted on having our own apartment before I would allow him to consummate the marriage.'

Her gaze wavered away and she dropped her head, shaking it sadly as she dragged out the core of her pain. 'Then three years ago . . . I fell in love with . . . with another man. So foolish and stupid! I didn't know what to do. There was no one I could talk to. No one who would understand what I felt, and not condemn me. Yet how can I be a good wife to Ahmed, when I love another man?'

Compassion stabbed through Ashley's heart. Her friend, trapped by custom into a relationship she didn't want, and loving . . . 'What about the man you love, Sohaila? Does he love you?'

She gave a sigh of utter misery. 'No! There was never any chance of that. He is an important man and I . . . he would not even see me as a woman to love. He was always nice . . . kind . . . that is all.'

The wretched yearning in Sohaila's voice convinced Ashley beyond a doubt that her friend was not in the grip of any shallow infatuation. 'Are you sure there's no chance with him, Sohaila? He might not have spoken because you were betrothed to someone else.'

Pain and the blackest of despairs looked back at her. 'It's Louis-Philippe! The Baron de Laclos. So you can see how hopeless it is, Ashley.'

And she did see. She could offer no consolation, no help. There was none. Louis-Philippe might be kind and chivalrous, but she had twice heard his opinion about cross-cultural relationships, and each time it had been delivered with negative overtones. She had no doubt that he liked Sohaila. Anyone who had worked with her for any period of time would have to grow fond of her. But Sohaila was right. Louis-Philippe would not see her as a woman to love.

And Ashley suddenly understood Sohaila's misery two days ago. That was when she had seen Louis-Philippe again after three years and known that she still loved him. It was savagely ironic that Ashley had gone to the casino that night in the hope of solving the problem of the marriage to Ahmed.

Sohaila's head lifted and her lovely eyes reflected the bleakness of her future. 'It was very kind of you, Ashley, to want to help us . . . to want to help me. And I am grateful to you. It makes me see where I am, what I have to do, no matter what my family says. I will have to break with Ahmed. I cannot continue the way I am going. I must be fair to him. At least he will be able to find someone else. There will be no disgrace on him.'

Ashley was well aware that an unmarried girl was considered a burden on the family in Egypt, and what Sohaila was proposing to do would probably make her a social outcast. It seemed so terribly unjust. And of what practical help could Ashley be? She would be going home to Australia soon. No wonder Sohaila had said she would miss her! Just when the Egyptian girl most needed a sympathetic friend . . .

The solution flashed into Ashley's mind like a lightning bolt. With Sohaila's ability and degrees, she could earn a good living anywhere in the world. Ashley snatched up her friend's hands, urgently pressing for her full attention.

'Sohaila, would you consider emigrating to Australia? I know my parents would sponsor you if I asked them. With your skills there would be no trouble getting a job. And you could come and live with me,' she suggested eagerly.

For a moment the sad, brown eyes lit with a glimmer of hope, but painful uncertainty quickly overshadowed it.

'Why not?' Ashley pressed. 'Is it such a frightening idea? If your family is going to make your life a misery, why stay on with them? You would be free to do anything you like in Australia, and you'd have no trouble making new friends in Sydney. I promise you, you wouldn't be lonely.'

Sohaila's gaze remained downcast and there was no discernible change of expression on her face. 'Ashley, you are so very good. Kind and generous to a fault. But I cannot make a decision now. Not until after I have done what I must.'

'I understand,' Ashley sympathised. 'Just remember you can count on my support, Sohaila. At any time. Are you going to speak to Ahmed tonight?'

She nodded.

'If either he or anyone else gives you a bad time, Sohaila, you walk out and catch a taxi to the hotel. Come up to my room. You're not alone any more. I'll be here for you.' Ashley suddenly remembered her dinner-date with Louis-Philippe and quickly added, 'If I'm not here, 'I'll leave my room-key at the reception desk for you. And think about coming with me to Australia. Will you do that?'

Uncertainty and need quivered over Sohaila's face. 'Thank you for caring so much, Ashley. You have given me the courage to do what I should have done twice before. I have never had someone who ...'

The tears welled up again, but they were tears of relief, and the two girls hugged each other with deep affection. Ashley had tears in her own eyes when Sohaila finally took leave of her and went bravely off to face the consequences of her decision.

Love is without mercy, she thought despondently. Louis had certainly been right about that. Damien's love for her ... Sohaila's love for Louis-Philippe ... and Azir's obsession with her—could it be called love? Could what she was feeling for him be called love?

Whatever it was, Ashley could not push it aside. If it was only desire, it was the strongest desire she had ever known. She wished for the courage to turn her back on every other consideration and take what Azir had offered.

It slowly dawned on Ashley that she had given that precise advice to Sohaila—to turn her back on everything she had known and emigrate to Australia. It had been so easy to say ... cheap talk ... costing nothing. Why couldn't she herself find the same courage as her Egyptian friend, who was about to break with a tradition that carried far greater penalties than Ashley would ever have to suffer?

She stared down at the money that was still scattered over the bed. It was Azir's money. She might have chosen the number, but he had put up the cash for the winning bets. It wasn't right to keep it, not now that the purpose for which he had given it to her was no longer valid. If she returned it to him . . .

Her heart skipped a beat, then careered around her chest in a wild thrumming of excitement. Her mind churned with all the possible consequences of such an action. The force of her agitation drove Ashley to pace up and down the floor.

She was mad to consider it! Mad! She had taken on the responsibility of Sohaila's plight. The sketches and the negotiations for the jewellery collection still had to be completed. Impossible to shirk either responsibility!

Would Azir let her go if she went to him? If she showed . . . if she said she did want him, that she wanted to know . . . needed to know all there was to know about him, to the depth of every intimacy possible between a man and a woman. A wanton wave of heat swept through Ashley, fanning the desire that was driving impulse towards resolution.

Azir had said he wouldn't make the same mistake again. He wouldn't keep her if she didn't want to stay. Ashley was certain he had been sincere when he'd said it. The risk was worth taking, anyway. There were no guarantees in this world. Anything could be taken away at any moment. Like Damien. Like her own life.

She was twenty-eight years old, with nothing ahead of her except her working career. And what was behind her? A marriage that had ended in guilt and grief, overshadowing its initial happiness. And after that, three years that had been barren of any meaningful relationships. Azir was right. She did want to taste him. She wanted to taste the best that life had to offer, and maybe this was her one chance to do just that. It was like the money she had gambled. It might win or it might not, but if she did not try, she would never know.

Ever since Azir had first touched her she had been running like a frightened gazelle. Wasn't she adult enough, mature enough, courageous enough to take one big step into the unknown? When she had come to Egypt she had been completely confident that she could handle anything that was thrown at her. The magnitude of the job in organising the jewellery collection had not daunted her; it had been a challenge she had eagerly accepted. Why should she shrink from the challenge of meeting Azir half-way?

Her gaze dropped once more to the money on the bed. In a burst of feverish activity she snatched up the wrapping from the box, wound it round the wads of notes and stuffed it into her large handbag. A self-conscious flush burnt over her skin as she stripped off her clothes and raced into the bathroom. It had been a long, long time since she had shared her body with a man.

She took a quick shower, all too aware of the tingling anticipation building inside her. Most of her clothes had been crushed from being packed in the suitcases, but she found a pretty floral blouse that was wearable, and teamed it with her good white skirt that always survived any mishandling. She brushed out her hair, dashed on her favourite *Joy* perfume, applied a soft pink lipstick; then, breathing as hard as if she had run a ten-mile race, she grabbed her bulging handbag and set off, determined not to retreat into cowardice.

The elevator took an age to come, and when Ashley eventually arrived on the ground floor more time was lost as she handed in her key at reception and left a message for Sohaila in case of unforeseen circumstances. The commissionaire compensated somewhat with the speed he summoned a taxi for her—a battered old Volvo this time. Ashley settled herself in the back seat and nervously gave her instructions.

'Take me to the Ibn Tulun mosque, please. I will give you further directions when we get there.'

The driver nodded and careered off into the traffic, horn blowing continuously at the cars whose drivers had the temerity to contest his right of way. With a sinking feeling of regret, Ashley remembered she had been too impatient to haggle over the fare. It was too late now, and she resigned herself to paying two or three times as much as she should.

They turned off Tahrir Bridge and edged down to Garden City with the driver keeping at least two cars within millimetres of his own all the way. Why more accidents did not occur, Ashley did not know. As soon as they left the main arterial road, she was again lost in the maze of narrow winding alleys that passed for streets. She breathed a sigh of relief when she saw the tall distinctive minarets of the old mosque.

The detailed memorisation of her first trip served Ashley well. The taxi-driver obligingly followed her instructions and within minutes they were at the gateway into Azir's house. Two uniformed soldiers with machine-guns guarded the entrance, and Ashley was instantly reminded of Azir's position of power. Such soldiers regularly patrolled the embassies and most of the big hotels as well.

A wave of panic glued Ashley to the back-seat. What if Azir wasn't here? What if . . .

'Ten pounds!' The taxi-driver was grinning triumphantly at her.

Ashley pulled herself together. If Azir wasn't here she didn't want to be left without transport in this place. She opened her handbag and passed over the money without argument. 'Please wait . . . five minutes,' she commanded, well aware that she had overpaid the man.

'I wait,' he said, still grinning, delighted at the prospect of picking up some more easy money.

Ashley screwed up her courage and alighted from the taxi. The soldiers gave her an interested appraisal, but did not challenge her passage through the gateway. The Arab guards at the entrance to the house were more particular.

They demanded her name, the nature of her call, and requested her to wait in the small vestibule until her admittance was accepted by the Sheikh. Ashley was so relieved to hear that Azir was at home that she did not mind waiting, but as the minutes ticked by, her inner tension grew.

The Arab who had effected her abduction swept in on her, and Ashley's heart fairly thundered with apprehension, but his courteous manner and speech eased her overstretched nerves. 'Please follow me,' he said, 'I am your guide.'

He escorted her through the house to what she now knew to be the men's quarters on the other side of the *qa'ah*. 'This is the library, *madame*,' he informed her as he ushered her into a large book-lined room. 'If you will wait here, the Sheikh will join you in a few minutes.'

'Thank you,' Ashley murmured.

He bowed and left the room, quietly closing the door behind him. Ashley took several deep breaths in an attempt to calm her skittering pulse-rate. She needed something to steady her trembling legs, so she walked over to the richly polished desk and propped herself against it. There were a number of comfortable-looking armchairs but the idea of sitting down had no appeal. To face Azir ... to say what she had to say ... she had to be on her feet. But she wasn't going to run from it. Not this time!

The soft click of the door-handle triggered a heightening of all her senses. Her eyes took in every enthralling detail of the man who entered. He had discarded his robes. In his white shirt and grey trousers he could have been any sun-tanned man on the streets of Sydney, except that he was still Azir. No one else she had ever met exuded that air of absolute power. And as he stood there, his dark gaze devouring every telling nuance of her appearance, Ashley lost all sense of purpose, except that of pleasing him.

He did not approach her. Nor did he speak. He waited, utterly motionless, a wary tension in every

still line of his body. Ashley knew it was up to her
to break the silence. She had rejected him three
times, and the memory of those rejections brought
a plunging loss of confidence. What if he rejected
her offer? What if he looked at her in contempt?
What if he said it still wasn't enough for him?
How would she bear the humiliation of being
refused?

'The money ...' The words burst forth before
she realised she had spoken them out loud. They
forced her to go on with other words of expla-
nation. 'I had to come and return it. My friend ...
I was wrong about her needing it. I thought it
would help her, but it wasn't the kind of help she
needed, so ...'

There was no reaction from Azir. His face was
completely impassive. He didn't move or speak.

Ashley fumbled open her handbag and drew out
the package of notes. Her hands were shaking. He
didn't come forward to take the money. He didn't
even glance down at it. His gaze did not move
from her, as if he was waiting, willing her to say
something he wanted to hear.

Ashley's heart was pounding in her ears as she
turned to place the packet on the desk. She had to
say it, and she had to say it now. Her courage was
slipping away and this would be her only chance.
She stared down at the parcel of money and forced
herself to speak.

'Why I came ... it wasn't only the money ... I
want ...'

Her voice dried up. Her head swam with the
buzzing urgency to choose the right words.

Everything sounded so cold and callous. Yet how could she express the turbulence of feeling he provoked? There was no other choice but to bluntly state what she felt. And she would face him as she did it!

Ashley lifted her head, straightened her back, then swung around to confront him. She met Azir's gaze with a proud defiance of any contempt he might feel for her. Her whole body was a quivering mass of vulnerability, but somehow she pitched her voice to a steady note of declaration.

'You were right, Azir. I do want you. And for the rest of the time I'm in Egypt, I want to be your lover.'

CHAPTER NINE

AZIR'S reaction was instant and explosive. The impassive mask split with sharp anger. A hard ruthlessness tightened his face, and an infinitely dangerous glitter flared into his eyes. His mouth thinned and curled with the cruel travesty of a forced smile.

'So you want me as your lover!' He threw the words back at her in a soft, ominous taunt. His hands lifted with slow, contemptuous deliberation, and began to unbutton his shirt. 'But only while you're in Egypt. And how long is that, Ashley? A few days? A week? A month?'

The light mockery gathered a vicious edge as he continued without giving her time to answer. 'I don't suppose it matters much. It's the satisfaction of the experience that counts, isn't it? Maybe the flesh of an Arab feels different. Maybe he does it a different way.'

He paused, one eyebrow raised in sardonic enquiry, but Ashley was too shattered to speak. The grain of truth in his interpretation of her words brought a scorching flood of shame to her cheeks. She had wanted to know what it would be like with him. She still did. She could not tear her gaze away from the hands that were steadily working down his shirt.

She wanted to say that it wasn't sexual

attraction that had brought her here, that there were other dimensions of feeling that he had stirred and left unanswered. But her mouth was completely dry, her tongue stuck to the roof of her mouth. The shirt was gaping open, revealing the muscular contours of a highly masculine chest; a sprinkle of tight black curls gave an intriguing texture to the darkly tanned skin.

'Would you prefer to undress me yourself?' he taunted, flicking his gold cuff-links through the cuff-openings.

The whip-sting in the observation forced Ashley's gaze up. The burning rage in his eyes stopped her heart in mid-beat.

'No? Then, let's not waste any more of your time.' He tore off his shirt and tossed it aside as he walked towards her, coiled menace in every step. He prised her handbag from her convulsively clutching fingers and hurled it into a corner of the room. 'You're not helping, Ashley. Do you want me to do everything?'

She was too stunned to move. His hands tore at the buttons of her blouse, impatient with her lack of response. 'Not ... not like this,' she croaked, finally forcing her voice to work.

'But this is all there is ... for you,' he retorted bitterly. 'But don't think I won't enjoy it, because I shall. I'll give you an experience you'll remember all your life.'

Her hands scrabbled up to snatch at his. 'Don't!' she begged, her eyes frantically pleading for understanding. 'You said we could only be lovers. That's why I came. I want to know you. To . . .'

'Oh, you'll know me, Ashley,' he promised, with no abatement of his fury. 'You'll know me to the very depths of your being before you leave Egypt.'

He grabbed the two opened edges of her blouse and pulled them down over her shoulders, dragging her arms back and keeping them imprisoned in the sleeves. To her intense humiliation, Ashley felt her nipples harden into knotted peaks as the hot afternoon air wafted on to her bared breasts.

'Please . . .' she whispered, her body already quivering its expectancy, her eyes desperately seeking some glimmer of mercy.

There was none.

'No?' he mocked, dropping the blistering heat of his gaze to the tremulous fullness of her breasts. 'I'm not to give you what you want? But we're so close, Ashley. Almost touching.'

He jerked her arms down, arching her back as he moved forward, his thighs pressing hers against the edge of the desk. The grip on her arms relaxed enough for her taut nipples to brush the prickling hair on his chest. Ashley gasped at the electric current. He rolled her upper body from side to side with a slow, deliberate, tantalising sensuality, inching her forwards, making her breasts ache to be crushed into the moist heat of his flesh.

And in spite of the hateful way he was using her, Ashley could not stop the insidious rise of sensual excitement. She almost groaned with relief when

Azir wrenched the blouse off her arms and caught her to him, crushing the breath out of her.

But there was no relief. One hand curved under her buttocks, pressing her lower body into his, working them both into a sexual arousal that was aggressively erotic. The hard thrust of him against her stomach excited Ashley beyond bearing, but he would not give her any freedom of movement. She could feel his heart thundering against her breasts and the heat of him soaked into her, melting any thought of trying to pull away. She wanted him, wanted him so much she didn't care what he thought of her.

'I could kill you for coming to me for this.'

The harsh whisper twisted her heart, but he gave her no chance to speak, to explain the need that had driven her here. Fingers threaded through her hair and dragged her head back. His face was contorted with violent emotion.

'I hate you for the way you're using me!'

'You don't understand!' Ashley cried, reaching up to hold his head still.

He looked at her with tortured eyes.

'I didn't meant to hurt you, Azir,' she whispered. 'I thought . . . we could try.'

'Try!' The word hissed from his lips and his eyes narrowed into glittering slits. 'Well, let's see how you like it, Ashley.'

One iron-tight arm pinned her to his body, while his other hand tore at the zip fastening at the back of her skirt. He hoisted her up and dragged both skirt and panties down over her hips.

'No!' she cried, beating down at his shoulders in frenzied panic.

'Yes!' he swore, and laid her on the desk so he could strip the clothes from her legs.

Her limbs seemed to have turned to water. Her arms flailed helplessly in her struggle to get up, knocking the pile of money she had placed so neatly on the desk into the air. Hundred dollar notes fluttered around her. She kicked out with her legs that were suddenly, frighteningly free of all constriction, and they were caught and relentlessly parted.

'No! No!' she panted, shocked by the melting weakness that trembled down her thighs. She couldn't find the strength to lever herself up. Appalled by the terrible vulnerability of her open nakedness she tried to squirm sideways, but a hand instantly spread across her stomach, defeating the movement.

'Please . . .' The word sobbed from her throat.

He removed the constricting hand, but only to pull her towards him. Ashley suddenly saw the full, vibrant power of his manhood and knew there was no escape even before his hands curled under her buttocks and lifted her.

'Yes!' he answered, his voice harsh with raging purpose as he thrust inside her, plunging hard and fast to the very centre of her being, finding it, filling it, then asserting his possession with a fierce stroking that ripped all thought from Ashley's mind.

Waves of pleasure-pain billowed through her, ebbing and flowing to the cataclysmic rhythm of flesh crashing into flesh. And Ashley found herself revelling in the sheer violence of this savage union, abandoning herself to it with a primitive exultation, abetting it by curling her legs around Azir's lean hips, tightening the pressure, urging him even more deeply inside her.

Her fingernails dug into the palms of her hands from the sheer frustration of not being able to pull him down to her. Her head threshed from side to side as tension built into wild urgency. Her whole body convulsed with the jerk of Azir's ejaculation, and she sobbed as she felt his power drain into limpness.

It couldn't be over, she wouldn't let it be over! It wasn't enough, it had to go on. Even as he removed the support of his hands and slumped forward, Ashley clung on to him with her legs. Her body acted instinctively, contracting the muscles necessary to imprison him within her. His head snapped up, a startled cry tearing from his throat, and Ashley felt a fierce jubilation at taking him captive. He arched back as if in denial, but Ashley would not let him go. With savage, wanton deliberation she rolled her thighs around him, her eyes feasting exultantly on the throbbing pulse-beat of his heaving chest, the incredulous shake of his head.

'No!' he groaned.

'Yes!' she hissed. 'Oh yes, Azir. You won't have it all your own way.'

His eyes glittered down at her, but it was no longer the glitter of rage. 'Do it, then. Have your own way!' he urged, his voice furred with challenging desire.

Excitement rippled through her. She had control this time. She would torment him as he had tormented her with his aggressive dominance. She didn't have to use strength. Just a seductive manipulation that kept him as her possession. She teased him unmercifully, moving from side to side, pressing the heat of her body against him, letting him slide a little then drawing him back in.

His breathing broke into ragged little gasps. His fingers raked her hips, across her stomach and down her thighs. Then with a frenzied cry, he gathered her up into his arms and crushed her to him, hugging her with a pressure that almost broke her in half.

Her legs started to slide down, but the stirring force of his loins pinned her to him, spearing inside her with a potency that made her gasp. Slowly, almost lovingly Azir lowered her to the desktop, gently supporting her with his arms. 'Until you're satisfied,' he promised huskily, then drew back, his eyes glowing with a warmth that made her tingle to her fingertips.

Ashley no longer cared what he did to her. She closed her eyes and clenched her hands, wanting to capture every nuance of feeling. A shudder of pleasure swept through her as he pushed past her womb. Excitement quickened with each stroke, some swift and certain, others slow and searching, but all driving her inexorably towards an explosion of exquisite sensation. And still he pushed on, spilling her from one orgasm to another, setting her afloat on a billowing sea of erotic pleasure that drained all the strength from her body.

A sweet, heavy languor invaded her veins. She did not know when Azir finally spent himself. She felt his arm slide under her shoulders. Another hooked under her legs. And then he was lifting her, cradling her against his chest, carrying her. His mouth brushed over her temples, whispering soothing words that she didn't understand.

It felt right that his arms were around her, the moist warmth of his flesh pressed to hers. Somehow she managed to lift her own arm, and curled it around his neck to hug closer, snuggling her face into his throat, breathing in his earthy male scent, tasting him with the tip of her tongue.

He groaned, his step faltering for a moment, then hurrying on. Ashley didn't look to see where he was taking her. She didn't care; didn't care about her nakedness, didn't care what he had in mind; didn't care about anything so long as he kept her with him. She vaguely heard the swish of silk curtains being swept aside, then Azir was bending over, laying her down, and there was cool satin beneath her, soft pillows under her head.

She opened her eyes and feasted on the glistening animal strength of his body as he slid down on to the bed next to her. He propped himself on his side to look down at her and she felt herself drowning in the dark whirlpools of his eyes. Love, tenderness, want, need; impossible to define the depth of emotion that pulled her to him, offering her mouth to his. He took it softly, without passion, but with a slow, erotic intimacy that was a possession of another kind; a sweet, shivery mingling of touch and taste and belonging.

The kiss went on, and on, and on; more intensely satisfying than any other in Ashley's experience, and her body shivered its pleasure to the soft caress of his hand. He circled her breasts, caressed her stomach, pushed slowly down to her thighs, slid up between them and held her there, gently sealing his claim on her. A delicious warmth pulsed through Ashley, and with it came a welling of emotion that brought tears to her eyes.

'I didn't hurt you?' Azir asked anxiously.

'No,' she whispered, her heart filling with contentment at the deep caring in his voice.

He sighed and rolled on to his back, pulling her with him so that her body half straddled his; her leg falling between the two strongly muscled thighs, her hip pressing against his manhood, her cheek resting over his heart. With half his body exposed to her touch, Ashley indulged the desire to run her fingertips over the powerful combination of firm flesh and muscle.

She thrilled to the sensitised crawling of his skin, to the slight shudders that followed the feathery paths she made. His chest heaved with the thunderous pounding of his heart and his hand raked up through her long hair, fingers entwining themselves in the long tresses, convulsively tugging, releasing, rewinding.

'Stay with me.'

The taut whisper stilled Ashley's hand. She felt his whole body tense as he waited for her answer. Even the fingers in her hair clenched together.

She wanted to say yes, yearned to say yes, *needed* to say yes, but she could not. If she were to live with Azir, she might never want to leave him. Not for any appreciable time. The burning sensation in her heart was proof enough of that. And she had to leave him. A week—a fortnight at most—and her work in this country would surely be finished.

She was pledged to follow through on the jewellery collection back home in Australia. That was her job, the responsibilty she had taken on. And her other responsibilities could not be shrugged away, either. Sohaila had her promise for help and protection; and Ashley herself had accepted Louis-Philippe's help. To throw every other consideration to the winds, and shut herself into a cocoon of existence that only recognised what could be shared with Azir, would be totally selfish and self-defeating.

Even if she could turn her back on everything else, what would her life be like if she stayed with him? They couldn't make love all the time. They had both acted out of sheer need for each other, and yet ... that didn't seem to matter in this blissful aftermath of togetherness.

It hurt to speak the words that would separate them, but Ashley could see no other way. 'I can't, Azir,' she said quickly, regret flooding through every fibre of her being. 'It's impossible, no matter how much I want to,' she added with even more feeling, and the deep sincerity of absolute truth.

There was no sound from him, no movement bar the almost imperceptible fall of his chest as he slowly exhaled pent-up air from his lungs. Then, with a stiff carefulness, the fingers in her hair spread open and pulled free of the tangled strands. His body remained quite still beneath her, but he no longer held her in any way. The message was chillingly clear. No words had to be spoken. She was free to leave. Right now, if that was her choice.

Regret savaged her heart and she pushed herself up to beg his understanding. Her eyes met a dark reserve that deflected her plea before it was uttered. 'I have appointments to keep, people I must see. And a friend who needs me to stand by her,' she stated, as matter-of-factly as she could.

The darkness of his eyes seemed to intensify, but when he spoke his voice was completely empty of tone. 'If you stayed here with me, you could come and go as you please. A car and chauffeur would be at your disposal. I will provide anything you require. Does that satisfy you?'

Her hands lifted in appeal, then fluttered limply in a gesture of hopelessness as Azir stared fixedly at her, waiting in judgement. To him the issue was obviously clear-cut, but it wasn't. Far from it. Her mouth twisted into a rueful grimace as she struggled to explain.

'That's extremely generous of you ... and I appreciate your ... your kindness ... but ... it's just not that simple, Azir.' She glanced down at her watch, suddenly realising that she had no idea how much time had elapsed. It was almost six-thirty. 'I have to go back to the hotel,' she murmured, more to herself than to him, but his reaction was cutting and abrupt.

'I'll get your clothes for you.'

He was on his feet and walking away from her before Ashley recovered her startled breath. 'Azir!' she called after him, but he had already strode through the opening of the curtains beyond the foot of the huge four-poster bed with its high canopy.

He did not reply to her call.

For the first time Ashley really looked at her surroundings. The three walls around her were richly covered in green and gold wallpaper. There were no windows and the room was smallish, containing a minimum of furniture. Elegant lamps stood on the two bedside tables. There were three Regency-style chairs upholstered in gold velvet. The only exit was the wall of gold curtaining that faced her.

Ashley swung herself off the bed and tiptoed to the opening, apprehensive about what lay beyond it. She gaped in startled surprise as her gaze drank in the luxurious furnishings that comprised what was obviously a private sitting-room and study. The room was huge; and the bedroom where Ashley stood was but a convenient recess at the end of it.

Desks, tables, cabinets and chairs, were all fashioned from heavily lacquered bamboo and decorated with chinoiserie motifs. Gold-framed mirrors and paintings hung on the walls and a magnificent crystal chandelier fell from the tall ceiling. She remembered Heba's enthusiasm over 'the English dining-room' but Ashley could not imagine its comparing to the Regency grandeur of this room.

The contrasts in Azir's house were as confusing as the man himself. He spoke English with a marked Oxford accent, but there was no diminution of his Arabic heritage. He was born a sheikh and would never be anything else, although Ashley fancied he would assert the innate power of his personal authority in any society. But was he really as cross-cultural as his possessions suggested? Would Azir ever accept a woman as an equal, or would he only regard her as a possession?

The questions were still teasing Ashley's mind when he re-entered the room, wearing the clothes he had discarded. He carried her sandals and handbag, and she could see her skirt and blouse hanging over his arm. Ashley shrank back from the curtain, feeling a self-conscious shame in her nakedness. Only her husband had ever seen her like this. It hadn't mattered while she and Azir had been close, but now . . . she snatched up a pillow in an instinctive need for protection.

Azir swept aside the curtain, and dropped her belongings on the bed. 'I trust you'll find everything there,' he said coldly, and without even glancing at her, left her to dress alone.

A terrible hollowness burrowed through Ashley's soul. Surely she did not deserve to be treated like a whore that he had finished with! But it was her own fault, she reminded herself savagely. As he saw it, she was using him in the same way, wanting him as a lover at her convenience.

Yet how could she commit herself into his keeping when . . . no, it couldn't be done! Their backgrounds were too different to even contemplate the total commitment she would want to give and be given.

Her hands trembled as she dragged on her clothes and tidied herself as best she could. A sickening regret weighed on her heart. But she could see no way of recapturing the precious intimacy they had shared.

It was some relief to find him waiting for her in the sitting-room. He was propped against a writing-desk, his arms folded, an impassive mask fixed once more on his face. 'I've ordered a car for you. It will take you back to your hotel,' he stated tonelessly.

'Thank you,' she murmured, the words almost choking on the rising lump in her throat.

His smile was a bitter twist of irony. 'You make a very impressive lover, Ashley. In fact, I've never had a better one. Please feel free to come at any time. I can't guarantee I'll always be available, but I'll do my best to accommodate you.'

His eyes slowly swept her from head to foot and back again in a taunting reminder of every physical intimacy there had been between them. Never before in her life had Ashley felt so shamed by her own words and actions. Pride urged her to say she would not come back, not ever, but in her heart she knew she would. She had to. She couldn't bear not to.

Her legs felt like half-set jelly but she forced them to cover the distance between them. Her eyes met his, honestly and openly, holding back nothing. 'It's not what you think, Azir. I don't

know where I'm going with you. I need time.
Maybe . . .'

His hands came up and gripped her shoulders.
She gasped as his fingers dug into her flesh, but
any hurt was seared away by the fierce passion that
blazed from his eyes. 'There's no . . . maybe . . . for
me, Ashley. Did you feel any . . . maybe . . . when
you gave yourself to me this afternoon? Did you?'
he demanded with bruising vehemence.

'No,' she whispered, enthralled with the
emotion that was bursting from him.

'It takes courage to give yourself completely to
another person, Ashley. To love so much that it
hurts to even think of being parted. You gamble
with your life, because you know the dependence
will be absolute and inescapable.'

He paused to drag in a deep breath, his eyes
swirling with dark torment as they searched hers.
His voice rasped between fierce conviction and
urgent demand as he added, 'Do you have that
courage, Ashley?'

What he appeared to be saying seemed so
unbelievable that the air caught in Ashley's throat
and choked her for a moment. A welter of
confusing thoughts sprang unbidden to her mind.
Was he really offering to share his life with her?
Completely? Without any reservation?

She stared up at him in terrible conflict;
her heart leaping with wild elation, her mind
desperately dictating caution. Her hand rose
spontaneously to touch the taut muscles along his
jaw-line, begging his patience while her eyes
pleaded for a stay in judgement. 'Please . . . Azir.

It's too soon. I don't know. I ...'

'How much longer will you be in Egypt?' His voice was harsh, demanding, discordant.

'Between one and two weeks. I'm almost finished. There's Aswan ...'

'Come back tomorrow,' he demanded.

'Yes!' she cried impulsively, driven into decision. Yet even as she spoke she remembered that Louis might have made some arrangement with the Egyptian officials. 'No, I can't,' she corrected swiftly.

The instant hardening of Azir's expresssion brought a stab of anguish. Her hands flew up around his neck, compelling him to listen. 'Please, Azir, you must understand. Tomorrow I've got the negotiations for the jewellery collection, and Louis ... the Baron de Laclos ... he is helping me, So ...'

'You go back to him?'

The hissed ferocity of the words stunned Ashley for a moment. Azir was snatching her hands down before she realised what he was thinking, and then her chest heaved with furious indignation at the bitter accusation in his eyes.

'I told you he was only a friend. I would never have come to you this afternoon if my ... my feelings were involved with him. If you don't know that, Azir, then you know nothing about me. You talk about love, but what about trust?' The turmoil he had put her through churned out more resentment. 'I've been as honest as I can be with you. If you can't ...' The anguish in her heart left her shaking her head in miserable despair. 'I knew it was impossible.'

'No!' Before she could move Azir had stepped forward and swept her against him in a crushing embrace. 'Nothing is impossible! It is up to you!'

His hand raked up through her hair and dragged her head back. She had a brief glimpse of his despair, then his mouth was on hers, passionately seeking what had been lost in the war of words. And Ashley could not fight the need that rose instinctively to answer his. She surrendered to it without the slightest hesitation, feeling the same violent desire for emotional reassurance.

They were both shaken by the tumult of passion that raged between them, and for a long time after the kiss ended they clung tightly to each other, too drained to speak or move.

'Forgive me my madness,' Azir finally murmured, his cheek rubbing softly across his hair. His chest rose and fell in a long sigh. 'I know I have to let you go, Ashley. I know this in my head, but my heart keeps crying out for you, and over that I have no control.'

He gently withdrew his embrace and lifted his hands to gently cup her face, his eyes openly pleading his cause. 'You must come back to me.'

'As soon as I can,' she promised, her own heart swelling with a blind surge of unquestioning love.

'Then go now, Ashley. Before I do or say something more I will surely regret.' A rueful smile played across his mouth as he released her. 'And I hope your business goes well for you tomorrow.'

'Thank you,' she whispered gratefully.

Ashley wished she could say more. She felt that Azir was doing all the giving, but she knew that if their relationship was to work, it needed the time and the understanding she had fought for.

He gently drew her arm around him. 'I'll take you down to the car.' As they passed the desk he picked up a card and pressed it into her hand. 'Ring that telephone number at any time, and I'll send a car to bring you here.'

'Thank you, Azir,' she murmured again, and she walked through his house with him, not even noticing the odd mixture of cultures, conscious only of the extraordinary man at her side.

CHAPTER TEN

ASHLEY was barely aware of the drive back to the hotel. She leaned her head back on the cool leather seat and closed her eyes, focusing her mind on all that had happened between herself and Azir. From almost the first moment she had seen him, her life had no longer been her own, and now ... now she simply couldn't comprehend a life without him.

He hadn't wanted her just for sex. It was more, much more than that. Ashley was certain of that now. When Azir had abducted her he had said he wanted her at his side for the rest of his life, and he had surely meant it. His words and actions this afternoon confirmed that beyond a doubt.

Ashley winced as she realised the terrible hurt she had given him in suggesting they be lovers while she was in Egypt. She hadn't meant that their relationship had to end then, but she now understood why Azir had reacted so violently. To have offered his life to her and then to be seemingly told he was only wanted as a short-term lover ... the insult to his pride had been deeply wounding.

Could she truthfully and confidently give him the commitment he wanted? Not yet, common

sense insisted. But her heart kept urging that it
didn't matter where their relationship was heading, or what heartache the future had in store for
them, she could not turn her back on it, nor choose
any other path. She wanted to be with Azir more
than she wanted anything else, and somehow she
had to work everything else out so that it was
possible to stay with him.

Ashley was forcibly jolted back to reality with
the car's arrival at the Sheraton. A glance at her
watch told her she barely had time to shower and
change before facing up to Louis-Philippe for
their dinner-date. She hurried through the lobby
and felt a surge of relief when she collected her key
and the receptionist informed her that Sohaila
Sha'ib had not called.

It was difficult to wrench her mind off Azir as
she soaped her body under the shower. Just the
memory of that wild act of intimacy in the library
was enough to stir involuntary spasms of pleasure.
She even hoped that Louis-Philippe's talk to the
authorities had been unsuccessful, so that her
departure from Egypt would be delayed as long as
possible. And that really was totally selfish, she
chided herself. Dewar and Buller would not be
impressed with such a lack of concern for their
interests.

And Louis-Philippe wouldn't appreciate that
attitude either, particularly since he had gone to
the trouble of involving himself on her behalf.
Ashley tried to get herself into a more responsible
frame of mind, but even by the time she was

dressed and presentable, her thoughts were still skittering around Azir.

The knock on her door brought her thumping down to earth. She took a deep breath. Louis-Philippe de Laclos was a man she liked and admired and respected, and he deserved her full attention. And her gratitude. She opened the door and smiled a welcome.

He was dressed in a beautifully tailored, dark grey suit and looked every inch a man of class; handsome, distinguished, impressive, a man of strong character and deep compassion. Ashley did not have to wonder why Sohaila had fallen in love with him. Few women could fail to appreciate so many attractive qualities, and he carried an individuality that successfully crossed all barriers.

'You look positively radiant, Ashley,' he said approvingly. 'I'm happy to see that yesterday's experience has not caused you any lasting trauma.'

Ashley winced at the thought of admitting the truth. A new zest for life was leaping through her veins, but it was because she had gone to Azir, not escaped him.

'Come in for a minute, Louis,' she said quickly, swinging the door wide open and waving an invitation for him to enter.

'How was your day?' he asked with friendly interest, accepting her invitation without question.

'Rather eventful,' Ashley admitted. 'I just have to write a note for Sohaila and leave it at the desk with my room-key before we go to dinner. If she decides to come here tonight ...'

'Sohaila? Why should she come?'

The sharp interruption cut Ashley's train of thought, then threw her into some emotional confusion. She could hardly confide Sohaila's problem to the man at the root of her friend's dilemma. 'It's ... it's a personal problem. Nothing to do with work,' she explained distractedly. 'Sohaila might be in trouble, and if she is I want to be available to help her.'

'So do I,' Louis-Philippe muttered with startling intensity. He crossed the space between them with a couple of strides and took Ashley's hands in a grip that was strong and rough and urgent. 'Why should Sohaila come to you tonight? What trouble is there that I don't know about?'

Ashley was dumbfounded by the sudden change in his manner. It vividly recalled the coiled tension of last night when he had faced Azir in the qa'ah, ready to fight to the death if necessary. Grim purpose was stamped on his face, and the steely glint in his eyes warned that he would not be diverted from that purpose.

'Ashley?' It was a terse reminder that she hadn't answered him.

'Sohaila went home to break her marriage contract with Ahmed,' she blurted out.

'To break ...' Shock and a curious conflict of emotions chased across Louis-Philippe's face. 'Why? After all this time?'

The questions weren't really asked of Ashley. He had withdrawn from her both mentally and emotionally, searching, struggling for answers that he could fit together himself.

A wild hope took root in Ashley's heart. It hardly seemed possible, but if there was any chance that Sohaila's love for Louis-Philippe was not unrequited, now was the time to clear any obstructions from their path.

'Sohaila doesn't love Ahmed. She never did,' Ashley said pointedly, watching to see what impact the information had on Louis. 'Only family pressure has kept her tied to him all these years,' she added for good measure.

Pain and despair ravaged his face as he dropped Ashley's hands and turned away, shaking his head. 'She can't do it! They'll make her an outcast, a social pariah. It'll be hell for her. She won't be able to stand out against them.'

He paced the floor in extreme agitation, and suddenly broke into a torrent of voluble French, which was too fast for Ashley to comprehend with her scanty knowledge of the language. She got the very firm impression, however, that it was the type of patois used by soldiers when they are very highly stressed.

Excitement lifted wild hope into the realms of probability. With slow, careful deliberation, Ashley set about clearing the path. 'I'm going to help Sohaila emigrate to Australia if she wants to. She had no one to turn to before, but she has now. Don't doubt her courage, Louis.'

He stopped in mid-stride, his head snapping back to her, his face appalled with the realisation that he had completely forgotten Ashley's presence. The strain to recompose his expression was evident, but within seconds he had brought himself under control. His hands even gestured an apologetic appeal as he spoke, but he could not quite strip his voice of the emotion churning through him.

'What I did for you yesterday, Ashley ... if Sohaila is in trouble I would have to do at least the same. She is ... very special to me ...'

Probability lifted into certainty and Ashley swiftly interrupted the spasmodic speech. 'Louis, we have been very frank with each other. Is Sohaila the reason you came back to Egypt? Do you love her?'

He grimaced at her bluntness, shook his head, then lifted eyes that were filled with helpless anguish. 'I would do anything for her, but ... Sohaila would never see me as a man to love. I am too old for her. More than twenty years older than her. And a foreigner.'

'Sohaila is deeply in love with you, Louis,' Ashley told him softly. 'It was seeing you again that forced her to realise she couldn't go through with the marriage to Ahmed.'

Still he struggled to contain the hope that Ashley had just held out to him, not quite daring to believe it after having lived through years of despair. 'Did Sohaila say that? Did she actually say ... she loved ... me?'

'Yes, she did. And cried her heart out because

she was sure you could never see her as someone you could love.'

A knock on the door froze them both for a moment. Then a sweet smile of satisfaction curved Ashley's mouth. 'If that is Sohaila, don't waste any more time, Louis.'

He muttered something in French, and the low, impassioned tone broadened Ashley's smile as she opened the door. Sohaila stood just outside, a suitcase in her hand, a look of frightened appeal working over her lovely face.

'You said ...'

Ashley reached out and took the suitcase; then caught her hand, giving it a reassuring squeeze. 'I said I'd be here for you, Sohaila, and I am. Come in. You're very welcome.'

The stiff apprehension eased enough for Ashley to pull her friend inside. She quickly shut the door, aware that Sohaila might be flustered into a retreat once she caught sight of Louis in her room. In her distressed state of mind she might leap to any number of wrong conclusions.

'Sohaila ...'

The soft call from Louis-Philippe carried an undertone of barely controlled emotion. Sohaila jerked around to face him, all colour draining from her face. Her mouth opened and closed. Her chest heaved as if fighting for breath.

'I ... I am sorry,' she said stiltedly, then darted an anguished look at Ashley. 'Please, I do not want to interrupt you, I ...'

'Sohaila!'

The urgency in Louis-Philippe's voice silenced her. Pain pinched her face, but she turned to him, squaring her shoulders and pasting a resigned dignity over her inner anguish.

He came forward and took her hands, his eyes glittering feverishly as he strove to contain himself. 'Do you know why I came back to Egypt?' he asked softly.

She lifted shy eyes to his and slowly shook her head.

His answer held an unmistakable throb of passion. 'Because you're here, Sohaila. Because I couldn't stay away. I had to see you one last time.'

The colour ebbed and flowed on Sohaila's face. She shot an agonised look at Ashley, desperately wanting to believe what Louis was saying, but afraid she was making some dreadful mistake. The words were too unbelievably wonderful to be fully credited on first hearing.

Ashley smiled her reassurance, then quickly picked up her handbag and room-key. 'I think you two have some talking to do in private. I'll come back later. Be happy.'

She felt like dancing down the corridor to the elevators. Louis-Philippe would surely look after Sohaila, and Sohaila would just as surely make Louis-Philippe happy. All the pain and suffering was over for both of them. In their case, love had triumphed against all the odds. The age difference, their nationalities, culture, religion . . . all had been swept aside by the purity of their feeling for each other.

And so it could be for Azir and herself, Ashley thought with happy determination. Being together was more important than anything else. Her delight for Sohaila and Louis was suddenly compounded by the realisation that the resolution of their problems also relieved her of worrying about them any more. She was free to go to Azir. Tonight if she wished. And she *did* wish! So strongly that it was almost a pain of need.

The card Azir had given her was in her handbag. One short telephone call to him and a car would be instantly despatched to the hotel. Within half an hour she would be . . . but she couldn't just leave without first saying something to Louis and Sohaila. They would worry about her. And she had to give them some time to reach an understanding before breaking in on them.

The elevator arrived and Ashley rode down to the first floor. Half an hour should be enough, Ashley decided, and she could fill that time in having something to eat. She had gone without food since breakfast time, and the Sheraton's La Mamma restaurant was one of the most pleasant dining-rooms in Cairo.

A waiter led her to one of the window-tables and took her order. Ashley settled back in the comfortable cane dining-chair, her gaze drawing pleasure from the clean whiteness of the furnishings, the bright touches of green and lemon, the thriving indoor pot plants. Like the sun-room in her parents' home.

The thought slid into Ashley's mind and stuck,

giving rise to other, less comfortable thoughts. Her parents would be appalled by what she was doing! They would never understand how she could throw up her career to go and live with a foreigner. When she went back to Australia to finish up her job, she would have to make up some story to account for her return to Azir ... taking up the offer to work overseas, or something like that. The truth would hurt them and she loved her parents too dearly to cause them worry and pain.

Yet how could she keep deceiving them indefinitely? She had taken no precautions this afternoon, and neither had Azir. If a child had been conceived ... the thought brought a warm tingle of happiness and suddenly it didn't matter what anyone thought. It was her life. She wasn't getting any younger, and she wanted Azir above all else. Sooner or later her parents would realise that her happiness depended on him and they would come to terms with the situation. They might never approve, but they would not condemn.

Ashley was certain that Azir would never turn his back on her or any children they might have together. Marriage was another question altogether, and one that Ashley wasn't ready to contemplate. She knew so little about Azir's life and the world he inhabited that she couldn't imagine how she would fit into it. But somehow she would. Azir no more wanted to be parted from her than she wanted to be parted from him.

The waiter brought the meal she had ordered, but Ashley was too churned up with the decisions she had made to enjoy it to any great degree. As she finished the last mouthful, a glance at her watch showed that ample time had passed since she had left Louis and Sohaila in her room. Ashley signalled the waiter, signed for the meal and left the restuarant. With her heart thumping in excited anticipation, she took the stairs to the reception lounge, then headed for a telephone.

It wouldn't take her long to pack. Even less time to wish Louis and Sohaila all the happiness in the world and take her leave of them. Sohaila could have her room. There was no reason for her to stay here at the hotel any longer.

She dialled the number on the card. Any time Azir had said, but it was not his voice that answered her call. Ashley calmed a sudden attack of nerves, gave her name, and asked to speak to Sheikh Azir Talil Khaybar, desperately hoping that he had not gone out somewhere.

'Ashley?'

A smile spread through her, relaxing all the tension. 'Azir, I can come to you now if you'd like to send your car for me. I'll have my suitcases ready in about fifteen minutes.'

She heard a quick expulsion of breath, then, 'I'll come for you myself.' Swift, decisive, and the line disconnected before Ashley could say anything else.

Not that it mattered, she thought joyously, as she skipped over to a miraculously open elevator and pressed the button for her floor. Azir was coming for her. In barely a quarter of an hour she would be with him again.

Ashley gave a discreet knock on the door of her room before using her key to enter, but she had no doubt that Louis would observe all the proper conventions where Sohaila was concerned. Sohaila would expect it, and Louis would respect her deeply ingrained sense of what was right and wrong. Marriage was the only answer that would satisfy their needs.

A rueful smile touched Ashley's lips as she opened the door, but she did not regret giving herself to Azir. Nor did she believe that she had lost any respect in his eyes. Neither of them had had any control over what had happened, and it had smashed barriers that might have otherwise kept them apart. Besides, as Azir had stated this afternoon, their relationship could only be that of lovers. Ashley had accepted that.

Louis and Sohaila were sitting on the bed, Louis holding her as if she were the most precious and fragile work of art. They were so wrapped up in each other that they weren't even aware that Ashley had entered the room.

Ashley cleared her throat. 'Can I assume that you two now understand each other?' she asked drily.

Sohaila leapt to her feet and flew over to Ashley, hugging her in rapturous happiness before drawing back to express herself more volubly. 'How can I thank you, Ashley? You are such a wonderful, wonderful friend.' Her beautiful almond eyes rolled all around their sockets in trying to express the intensity of her emotion, and her hands flew into any number of eloquent gestures.

'Oh, perhaps you could name one of your daughters after me,' Ashley replied teasingly, and laughed as a bright red flush stained Sohaila's cheeks.

'If we are blessed with a daughter, we will do that, Ashley,' Louis said seriously, standing up and curving a loving arm around Sohaila's waist. 'We will always be grateful to you for bringing us together.'

Sohaila looked adoringly into eyes that had lost all trace of sadness. 'Louis is going to speak to my parents.' She dragged her gaze back to Ashley. 'He says he will smooth over all the trouble. But we will get married anyway,' she declared with triumphant defiance.

'And very soon,' said Louis.

'Good for you,' Ashley approved warmly, and kissed them both in benevolent blessing.

She had no doubt that Baron Louis-Philippe de Laclos would find a way to appease the Sha'ib family, but Sohaila's declaration of love and loyalty to the Frenchman was an assurance that nothing would stand in the way of their being together. Ashley hoped they would both understand her own decision.

'I've just telephoned Azir,' she announced. 'He'll be here in about ten minutes and I'm going to ... to live with him.' There was no point in mincing words, Ashley told herself sternly, and continued in a calm, steady voice. 'So you can have my room, Sohaila.'

'The Sheikh?' Sohaila's eyes widened incredulously.

Ashley nodded and turned to open her suitcases. 'I know you'll probably find it shocking, but it's what I want, Sohaila, and my life is my own to do with as I want.'

A touch on her arm drew her out of the wardrobe she had opened. Sohaila's lovely dark eyes brimmed with emotion. 'I know you could only be following your heart, Ashley. I would never think badly of you whatever you did. Ever,' she said with loyal fervour.

Ashley nodded, too choked to speak. She didn't know why it meant so much to her, but she was intensely grateful for Sohaila's support.

'Now let me help you pack,' Sohaila continued, showing her uncritical acceptance of Ashley's decision.

'Ashley, is there anything I can do for you?' Louis asked, a worried note in his voice.

She took a deep breath to clear the lump in her throat and shook her head. 'Did you get anywhere with talking to the authorities about the jewellery collection?' she asked belatedly.

'Progress has been made, but of course they did not commit themselves,' he said dismissively. 'I meant . . . what if you are not happy with Azir?'

She flashed him a smile to appease his concern. 'I'll face that problem when it comes—*if* it ever arises. Don't worry about me, Louis. I was frightened of Azir yesterday, but not any more.'

Louis nodded, but his concern deepened into a dark frown. 'I hope you understand what you're doing, Ashley.'

A tremor of fear ran through Ashley's heart. Was she risking too much?

'Louis...' Sohaila's lilting voice held a soft note of indulgence '... I do not think you understand how it is. Ashley would not go to him if she ever meant to leave. And the Sheikh ... he cares very much, or he would not have come with the money this afternoon.'

Louis frowned in puzzlement. 'What money?'

'I will tell you later,' Sohaila assured him. 'For now you must wish Ashley happiness, not worry her with doubts.' A chiding smile curved her mouth. 'You know, Louis, sometimes you men make it very hard for us women.'

His answering smile begged forgiveness. 'I will learn from my mistakes. Ashley, I wish you all the happiness that you've made possible for me, and for ...'

'... me,' Sohaila breathed gratefully.

And Ashley hugged their blessing to her heart, all too aware that happiness could be snatched out of one's grasp with a mere twist of Fate. She had lost Damien; Louis and Sohaila had very nearly lost each other. Determination swept all doubts aside. She was *not* going to lose Azir.

CHAPTER ELEVEN

ASHLEY had planned what she would say to Azir but, as in all their encounters, he took control the moment he arrived at her hotel room. His eyes blazed at her with a fierce possessiveness that seared away all coherent thought, and his kiss left her quivering with an excitement that blotted out every other consideration. A porter took care of her luggage and Azir swept her out of the hotel and into his car before Ashley recovered enough to speak.

'Thank you for coming,' she said huskily.

Azir's fingers threaded hers and gripped tight. He looked at her, and that one look cut staight through conventional speech even before he spoke. 'It was agony ... waiting for your call.'

His pain shamed her, reminding her of the times she had rejected him. 'I'm sorry. It won't happen again, Azir.'

'You will stay with me now?'

'Yes.'

Her answer was unequivocal, drawn from her by the intensity of feeling emanating from Azir. The moment was so charged with tension that Ashley postponed explaining the necessity of a return trip to Australia. She didn't even want to think about it. Azir's dark eyes were devouring her again, and the desire flooding through her veins weakened any sense of purpose beyond pleasing him.

When they arrived back at the house, Ashley was once more installed in the Damascus Room with Heba in fluttering attendance. The servant-girl was delighted that this time she was allowed to unpack the suitcases and see to all Ashley's needs. And when finally she was dismissed by Azir, the ensuing silence in the room throbbed with too much urgent anticipation to even think of words.

Their lovemaking was a raging tempest of desire, totally demanding and intensely satisfying. The violence of their need for each other gradually eased into a sensual tenderness that savoured their mutual possession in a slow, knowing celebration of absolute intimacy. For a long time they lay together in a silence of blissful harmony.

'Ashley ...'

The soft whisper of her name carried an undertone of need that stirred Ashley out of her sweet languor. Suddenly there was something different in the stillness of Azir's body, a tension in the prompting pressure of his fingertips.

'Yes?' she asked quickly.

'You accept now ... that we belong together?'

It was too dark for any telling expression to be seen on Azir's face, or in his eyes, but the tight cautiousness in his voice was warning enough that her answer was very important to him.

'Yes,' she said, with careless disregard of the consequences. It was the truth. Not even with

Damien had she felt such a deep sense of belonging. She no longer questioned why Azir should have the power to bind her to him, and there was no point in denying it. She took a deep breath and told him her decision. 'When my business here is finished, I will have to return to Australia for a short while to tie up my commitments there. But if you want me to, I'll come back and live with you, Azir.'

His fingers dragged up and down her back. 'If . . .' He breathed the word as if he hated it. He moved abruptly, heaving himself up to lean over her. 'Do not speak of "ifs" again, Ashley. Have I not made it clear what I want?'

There was anger and frustration in the way he kissed her, and Ashley's passionate response did nothing to soothe either emotion. 'How can you leave me?' he demanded, his breathing harsh and spasmodic as he continued, 'Do you not feel as I do? I say that you cannot go. I will not permit you to leave me.'

Shock squeezed her heart. She had not anticipated that Azir would try to force his will on her again. As she stared up at him in stunned confusion, he gave a groan of anguish and shook his head.

'No, I do not mean that. You are free to do what you like. But for your return to Australia, you must accept that I cannot let you go alone. Now that you have come to me, Ashley, I cannot bear to be separated from you. The thought of not having you constantly by my side . . .'

'You'll come with me?' she cried, relief heading the surge of happiness that washed through her.

'You don't object?'

The pained uncertainty in his voice brought a choking lump of emotion to Ashley's throat. She didn't care what her parents or anyone thought. 'I'd love you to come with me, Azir. I don't want to be separated from you either.'

His chest heaved as if he could no longer contain the emotion swelling his heart. 'I love you, Ashley. More than life itself. Won't you reconsider about only being my lover?'

Before she could reply, Azir continued, the words spilling from his tongue in passionate bursts. 'I want you, I need you, I love you. Please, my darling, I want you to think about being my wife. You tell me we are too different, that it is impossible. But that is not so, and I will prove it to you. Ask what you like of me, and if it's within my power, I will give it to you ...'

Joy ripped away the shock. Ashley hadn't dared let herself hope for so much, but Azir surely meant what he was saying. He did not want her as his mistress, but as his wife!

'... You said you needed time, and I will not press you, Ashley.' He hurried on. 'I do not expect you to love me with the intensity I love you. Just give me the chance to show you that our lives can be melded together, and I will do all I can to make you happy. I need you so much, so ...'

She reached up to kiss the words of love flowing from his mouth. He stopped the violent outpouring of emotion to take the sweet offering of her mouth with a passionate intensity that even more eloquently transmitted his need for her.

It was minutes later that he broke away from the thraldom of her response. 'You will think about it, then?' he demanded hoarsely.

'Yes. Oh, yes!' she breathed happily. 'I don't understand it. I still hardly know you. But I've never felt this way about a man before. I . . .'

His hands trapped her face, stilling her speech as he struggled to accept the words she had spoken. 'Ashley . . .' It was a plea, a wish, a clutch at a dream he had not dared believe in. His voice gravelled along the edge of hope. 'Oh, Ashley, do you really mean what you're saying?'

'Yes,' she said simply, giving him the most direct reassurance.

A cry of elation broke from his lips. 'Then it will be all right. You will see, my darling. I will make you so happy . . .'

He rained passionate kisses all over her face, down her throat, and Ashley hugged him to her with a fierce thrill of possessiveness. However foreign and alien he had once seemed to her, he had brought her back to a life worth living and she loved him. She loved him!

On that sweet wave of certainty she spoke. 'I don't have to consider it, Azir . . .'

'No!' The breath was squeezed out of her as Azir caught her to him in a crushing embrace. 'You can't deny me. We are meant for each other. From the first moment I saw you . . . Ashley, you must have felt it too?' he cried despairingly.

'Yes,' she confessed. 'And I will marry you, Azir. That's what I was going to say.'

The expulsion of a tortured breath whispered through her hair, and then he was lifting his head and Ashley felt the exultation that soared through him. 'You will be ... my wife?'

A totally primitive satisfaction ripped through Ashley at the ring of ecstatic ownership in those last two words. 'Yes,' she breathed, knowing on every instinctive level that this man was her mate and there would never be another.

He touched her face, almost in wondering reverence. 'I have been waiting for you, wanting you all my life. I cannot describe ... you cannot conceive the despair I felt when I found out you were married. And when you left with the Baron ...'

She brushed his mouth with soft, silencing fingertips. 'I promise you I'll never leave you again, Azir. I'm sorry I hurt you so much.'

He took her hand and pressed her open palm against his cheek. 'No matter now. I promise that I will never give you cause to regret this, Ashley.'

She smiled. 'How could I? I love you.'

He kissed her with a worshipful tenderness that brought tears to Ashley's eyes. They trickled down her cheeks and Azir's mouth roved lovingly over her face, kissing away the salty stains, murmuring huskily against her skin, 'You must not weep, Ashley. I will always be by your side to look after you. I will not let anything come between us.'

She remembered his ruthlessness in pursuing her and did not doubt his claim. And she remembered also how he had tempered that ruthlessness, loving her so much that he would not make her unhappy by taking her freedom away. He had conceded her the right to choose, against his own interests, and she loved him all the more for it.

Whatever differences there were between them didn't matter. She believed, as Azir said, that nothing would come between them, nothing that could make her regret the decision she had made tonight. The commitment had been given, he to her and she to him, and when Ashley finally dozed off to sleep in the arms of her lover, she was absolutely positive that she was where she wanted to be. With Azir for the rest of her life.

CHAPTER TWELVE

THE next few days were the most exciting Ashley had ever experienced. She grew to appreciate what a multi-cultural man Azir was, with so many impressive facets to his character that she was almost in awe of him. Why he loved her, of all the women who had crossed his path, she couldn't imagine, but she was intensely grateful that he did, and he never left her in any doubt of it.

Each day seemed to bring them closer together, nearer to a perfect union of a man and a woman, closer to a total acceptance of each other for exactly what they were. Ashley could only shake her head in wonder whenever she recalled Azir's certainty that first night they had met. 'The bond is already forged,' he had declared, and he had been right. And the bonding grew stronger with every minute they spent together.

There were hours in every day when they had to be apart, Ashley to conclude her business, Azir on affairs of state. The rapture of finding each other, whether it was in the Chinese Room, or the Regency Room, or any other room, was like a reuniting of two separate streams of life which were totally diminished without the other.

As for her negotiations over the jewellery collection, once Azir heard of her problems, he immediately swung his influence behind her. Louis-Philippe had been helpful, but it was Azir who opened doors for her that would always be shut to foreigners. The negotiations had quickly progressed to the stage where her firm's proposals had been accepted in principle, and that virtually concluded Ashley's mission in Cairo.

It gave Ashley enormous satisfaction to send all the completed paperwork back to the company management in Australia. Mr Buller, who had been responsible for sending her to Egypt in the first place, would now handle all future developments. There was only the Aswan trip to be made for her portfolio of sketches to be completed also, but Ashley was reluctant to leave Azir, even for a few days.

However important she had once thought the Egyptian Collection to be, her work on it certainly didn't rate at all if it meant she and Azir had to be separated. She even contemplated asking Mr Buller to send a replacement for her, but in the end common sense prevailed. She had taken on a job and her own sense of reponsibility demanded that she finish it.

When she told Azir she should make the trip, he nodded thoughtfully then asked, 'How many days do you need in Aswan?'

'Three or four, I suppose,' she answered regretfully. 'I'll be as fast as I can.'

The dark eyes lit with delight at her eagerness to return to him. 'I will go with you, Ashley. My business here can wait. Our time together is far too precious to waste.'

Ashley flew into his arms, hugging him in happy relief. 'You're sure it will be all right? You mustn't let my work interfere ...'

'I will make it right,' he said, with an arrogant assurance that Ashley no longer resented. She had come to the conclusion that Azir could make just about anything happen if he set his mind on it. He really was the most extraordinary man.

'However,' he continued, his eyes searching hers in concern, 'I am not sure that it's a good thing, your giving up your work, Ashley. It has been part of your life for so many years. If you begin to miss it, you must tell me, and ...'

She laughed in sheer happiness. 'Oh, Azir! I doubt I will have time to miss it. I think running your homes in Paris and London and Rome and Washington will be a full-time job, not to mention being the wife of a very busy diplomat. And I'm going to love every minute of it.'

She kissed him to erase any possible doubt in his mind, and he smiled his contentment. 'As long as you are happy, Ashley. But remember, I will arrange whatever you want.'

Ashley didn't doubt that he would. There was nothing mean or selfish in Azir's regard for her. Her happiness was his first concern, and he proved it over and over again.

They flew to Aswan in his private jet and Azir devoted all his time to her, never leaving her side, and even taking a keen interest in the jewellery that Ashley pointed out to him as designs that were unique to this region. He insisted on buying her a silver bracelet that was a particularly fine piece of workmanship, and would have bought her more if Ashley hadn't vigorously protested.

The days passed all to quickly; bright, scintillating days of blissful companionship, and nights of long, passionate lovemaking. On their last night in Aswan, it was very late when their desire for each other was finally sated. Ashley awoke early the next morning, her subconscious mind restless with the knowledge that her work in Egypt was finally finished. They would be going to Australia soon. She hoped that her parents would welcome Azir when she introduced him to them.

Azir was still asleep and it was Ashley's first experience of actually seeing him in complete repose. Invariably he woke first in the mornings, and it was his loving caresses that drew her out of sleep. She was tempted to do the same to him, but there was a touching vulnerability in his stillness that gave her pause for thought.

There was one other matter that had to be sorted out before she left Egypt. Ashley had been putting it off, not wanting to raise an issue that might bring discord into the wonderful harmony of their own personal happiness, but she had to speak to Azir about Louis-Philippe and Sohaila.

Friendship demanded it.

Azir had been more than good to her. Nothing that could please her was too much trouble or too expensive. Ever since she had gone to live with him he had been showering her with an embarrassment of gifts. He was incredibly generous, but what she wanted to ask might test his generosity too far.

She loved Azir too much to hurt him. A sigh of sweet contentment whispered from her lips as her gaze travelled slowly over his firm, muscular body, and a smile curved her mouth as she noticed the curly thickness of his long, black eyelashes. She hoped their child would inherit them.

Ashley's hand crept over her stomach, hugging her secret pleasure in the knowledge that her monthly period was late. Only a few days late. Not long enough to be absolutely positive about a pregnancy. But in her heart Ashley was certain that a child had been conceived.

A vague sense of guilt flitted through her mind as she thought of Damien, who had so desperately wanted her to have his child. He had been a good and wonderful person, a truly loving partner, yet Azir had given her a joy in loving that she had never experienced before. There was no way Ashley could compare them, nor did she want to. Damien belonged to the past now, and there was nothing more she could do for him, ever. Azir was her present and her future, and Ashley was determined to make whatever adjustments were necessary to keep their life together happy.

But could Azir make the emotional adjustment necessary to accept Louis-Philippe's company? Ashley reached out a hand to touch him, then withdrew it, reluctant to disturb him when he looked so relaxed and peaceful.

Very carefully, she slid out of bed and padded over to the window that gave such a spectacular view of Aswan. She wanted to imprint it on her memory before she left, because she was quite sure there could be no place in the whole world that encapsulated so many contrasts.

Their rooms were on one of the top floors of the Oberoi Hotel on Elephantine Island in the middle of the Nile River. Below her, the gardens leading up to the hotel from the ferry wharf were lushly tropical, and the green strip of fertility along the banks of the Nile held masses of palm trees; yet the harsh backdrop of the sterile desert was a telling reminder of how precious water was in this ancient land.

Along the city-side bank of the river, a row of modern cruise-ships stood at anchor, waiting for their fill of tourists before beginning the journey down to the Valley of the Kings near Luxor. The island harbours held a fleet of *feluccas*, the sturdy, primitive sailing-boats that had been in service for many hundreds of years, their swift manoeuvrability still shaming modern technology.

On the west bank of the Nile stood the luxurious villas built by the Aga Khan; behind it like a lonely sentinel in the desert his marble tomb; on the east bank the poverty of the Nubian dwellings, and the granite quarries that had provided the outer casings for the pyramids of the Pharoahs.

Further up the river, although it was too far away for Ashley to see it, was the High Aswan Dam. Azir had taken her to look at it, intent on explaining all the problems that had to be taken into consideration with every step towards modernisation in these third world countries. Although the dam regulated the flow of the Nile so that there was no more destructive flooding, the valley no longer received deposits of rich silt, and the soil was losing its fertility.

Ashley no longer worried about the differences between her and Azir's backgrounds. Despite the kind of contrasts in their lives that she saw spread below her in Aswan, nothing could change what they had together.

Ashley had been so deep in thought she hadn't heard Azir get out of bed, and she gasped in surprise when his arms slid around her. She nestled back against him, loving the feel of his warm, hard flesh pressing into hers. He trailed little kisses over the curve of her shoulder and she twisted her head around to smile at him.

'What were you thinking of?' he asked, rubbing his cheek against hers with a sensual tenderness that sent a warm ripple of pleasure right to her heart.

'Lots of things,' she sighed, and turned around

into his embrace.

She looked up into eyes that searched hers intently. 'Going home?' he questioned.

'Home is where you are, Azir,' she answered, and kissed him with all the passionate conviction in her soul.

He clung on to their togetherness, his arms encircling her in compelling ownership. 'I thought you might have been a little homesick for Australia. And your family. When I meet with your parents, Ashley, I will assure them that I shall care for you always. They may or may not approve of me, but at least they will know I am sincere in my love for you.'

Happiness overflowed from her heart and her eyes sparkled their contentment. 'They will approve! How could they not approve when you make me so happy?'

He laughed. 'So when do you want to leave Egypt? I have already begun making arrangements to take temporary leave, but I need to have a date of departure.'

There was no time to think of a tactful way of approaching the question she wanted to raise. 'It depends on you, Azir. Sohaila and Louis-Philippe have invited us to their wedding. The marriage ceremony is to be held in a fortnight's time. I know you ...'

'If we attend the ceremony, you will stay in Egypt an extra fortnight. Is that what you are saying Ashley?'

Ashley sighed, feeling she was defeated before she had barely begun. 'I know that you and Louis-Philippe can never be friends, but Sohaila is very dear to me, and . . .'

'. . . and we will go to the wedding!' He frowned over the uncertainty he heard in Ashley's voice. 'Don't think of me as being some form of tyrant, Ashley. An Arab is not the same as a Western man. Our wives are our dearest possessions, partners in life, sharing everything. Marriage is for ever. Of course I will go to the wedding with you. I will always consider what you want, and give you all that it is possible for me to give.'

Ashley shook her head in wonder at the faultless generosity of the man she loved. She felt uniquely blessed that he loved her. 'Thank you, Azir,' she said with heartfelt gratitude. 'I realise what it must cost you, with all the enmity between your family and his. It's more than I ever expected . . .'

He smiled, his eyes caressing her in a way that made Ashley prickle with pleasure. 'Perhaps it is time to put enmity aside,' he said softly. 'We were born on different sides of the fence, born to fight one another, but I do not forget that my father owes his life to the Frenchman.'

The smile tilted into dry irony. 'The Baron is a man of courage and integrity. I'll grant him that. And now that we are no longer involved in battle over you, my love, I can view him far more tolerantly than I ever could before. It is even possible that we could come to understand each other, so I'm not averse to meeting him. Particularly since it pleases you.'

Ashley could not stop the wide grin that spread across her face. These two extraordinary men shared so much more in common than they would ever realise. 'I think you will like Louis, once you get to know him, Azir.'

He laughed. 'Perhaps. One thing is certain—I am obliged to him if going to his wedding will keep us a fortnight longer in Egypt. Now that we are being married there is much to be arranged, and I prefer to do it in a civilised manner.' His eyes gathered a gleam of possessive desire as he added, 'Not that anything would stop me from marrying you, or going with you to Australia. I have a terrible need for you, Ashley.'

'Now?' she teased, sliding her arms around his neck and swaying provocatively against him.

'Now,' he growled, and swept her back to bed where he made love to her for a long time, until they found a mutual peace in each other's arms.

They lay together, gently caressing in the soothing afterglow of total contentment. Instinctively responding to the need to share everything, Ashley snuggled closer as she prepared to tell her husband-to-be that she might be carrying his child.

'Azir ...' she whispered, trying to contain her own excitement, and hoping he would be just as pleased as she was. 'I think you might have become a father.'

'I tried hard,' he agreed, and she looked up to see a triumphant grin on his face. 'I've been trying hard ever since you came to stay with me,' he confessed. 'I know you won't change your mind now, Ashley, but I wanted to be sure you would marry me one way or another.'

Ashley laughed out of sheer joy. 'Well, I think you succeeded on the first day, because I . . .'

The grin went slack as he stared up in surprise, then gently pressed her back on the pillows, a whole range of emotions skating across his face. 'Ashley, you don't mean . . . already?'

'Do you mind?' she asked, a chill of apprehension rippling over her heart as she saw the dazed horror in his eyes.

'You should not have let me make love to you so . . . so violently,' he choked out. 'If we have hurt the baby . . .'

She barely swallowed a bubble of laughter as relief swept through her. 'It can't possibly have hurt the baby, Azir.'

His relief was slower in coming. 'Are you sure?'

'I'm sure,' she said, very positively.

A smile of absolute pleasure lit his face. He caressed her lazily for hours, kissing her breasts and stomach, loving her for the mother she was going to be. Ashley lay in his arms, finding pleasure in giving pleasure, knowing that a whole new way of life was opening up for her . . . the wife of a diplomat . . . mother of a child . . . perhaps of several children, if Azir wanted them. Clearly, the idea of being a father was very much to his taste.

She thought how strange it was that love could change so many perceptions, so irrevocably alter a person's life. Sohaila's and Louis-Philippe's also, not just hers and Azir's. So much had been changed since that first night when she had gone to the casino to win the money for Sohaila. And Azir had won it for her. She remembered her incredulous shock when the number she had chosen had in fact come up.

'Azir,' she said drowsily as his mouth moved adoringly down her body.

'Mmm?'

'You're a very lucky man!'

He moved his head sideways, and looked back at her consideringly. 'That is exactly so! I never thought otherwise.'

'You misunderstand me,' Ashley laughed back. 'I'm not so conceited as to think you're lucky to have me. What I meant was the first time we met. You remember?'

'How could I ever forget it?' His voice was deep with pleasant memories.

'You had the luck of the devil himself on that roulette wheel. I even thought so at the time. Particularly with that last bet on twenty-three. I thought you were mad to do it, but ...'

She stopped, intrigued by the odd shift of expression on his face; a look of guilt, then remorse, and finally a touch of self-mockery. 'Ah, Ashley,' he sighed, then took the bit between his teeth and plunged on. 'Don't ever believe in that kind of luck.'

'But ... I saw you have it,' Ashley protested, puzzled by his reaction and assertion.

His mouth turned down into a grimace. His eyes begged her understanding. 'Sometimes in the diplomatic service it is necessary to make an impression. We have ways ... it's not really diplomatic to say what they are ... it costs a great deal of money ...'

'Azir, are you trying to tell me that ...?'

'My dearest darling, you must not question me! There are some things that are best not revealed. Believe me! All I'm trying to suggest to you is that you should never trust in luck.'

Ashley let the information filter through her mind. He had not won the money. She was quite certain of that. He had wanted her so badly he must have paid for whatever he won. She remembered what he had said at the time. 'I don't gamble. And I always win.'

And he had certainly won her, Ashley thought in another burst of ecstatic happiness. She wound her arms around his neck. 'Thank you for loving me, Azir,' she said fervently, and it was a prayer of gratitude for all he had done for her, and a paean of praise for the life ahead of them.

'How could I not?' he replied simply. 'We were made for each other.'

And Ashley knew he was right. Even when her mind had denied it, her instincts had recognised the truth. Whatever the odds had been against them, they had found each other, and the bond had been forged.

Step into a world of pulsing adventure, gripping emotion and lush sensuality with these evocative love stories penned by today's best-selling authors in the highest romantic tradition. Pursuing their passionate dreams against a backdrop of the past's most colorful and dramatic moments, our vibrant heroines and dashing heroes will make history come alive for you.

Watch for two new Harlequin Historicals each month, available wherever Harlequin books are sold. History was never so much fun—you won't want to miss a single moment!

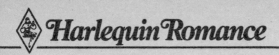
Harlequin Romance

Coming Next Month

2947 BENEATH WIMMERA SKIES Kerry Allyne
Mallory is tired of her international jet-set modeling career and
wants only to manage the outback ranch where she grew up.
Unfortunately, Bren Dalton, the man with the say-so, doesn't think
Mallory capable of it.

2948 SEND ME NO FLOWERS Katherine Arthur
Samantha has doubts about ghostwriting Mark Westland's memoirs,
despite the elderly actor's charm. And when it brings Blaize
Leighton to her door, determined to keep his mother's name out of
the book, her life becomes suddenly complicated....

2949 THE DIAMOND TRAP Bethany Campbell
A schoolteacher's life is thrown off balance when she chaperones a
young music prodigy to Nashville—and falls for the very man she
came to protect her student from! And what about her fiancé back
home?

2950 YOU CAN LOVE A STRANGER Charlotte Lamb
Late-night radio disc jockey Maddie enjoys her life in the quiet
seaside town—until Zachary Nash, a stranger with an intriguing
velvety voice, involves her in a tangle of emotional relationships
that turn her life upside down!

2951 STRICTLY BUSINESS Leigh Michaels
Gianna West and Blake Whittaker, friends from childhood, now
senior partners in a cosmetics company, have known each other too
long to cherish romantic notions about each other. Or so Gianna
believes—until a glamorous rival causes a change of mind...and
heart.

2952 COLOUR THE SKY RED Annabel Murray
As a writer of horror stories, Teale Munro works very unsocial
hours, and he assumes Briony, as an artist, will understand why he
feels able to offer her only an affair. Except that he badly misjudges
Briony and her feelings....

Available in December wherever paperback books are sold,
or through Harlequin Reader Service:

In the U.S.
901 Fuhrmann Blvd.
P.O. Box 1397
Buffalo, N.Y. 14240-1397

In Canada
P.O. Box 603
Fort Erie, Ontario
L2A 5X3

Harlequin Romance

Enter the world of Romance...
Harlequin Romance

Delight in the exotic yet innocent love stories of
Harlequin Romance.

Be whisked away to dazzling international capitals... or
quaint European villages.

Experience the joys of falling in love... for the first
time, the best time!

Six new titles every month for your reading enjoyment.
Available wherever paperbacks are sold.

Harlequin American Romance

Romances that go one step farther...
American Romance

Realistic stories involving people you can relate to and care about.

Compelling relationships between the mature men and women of today's world.

Romances that capture the core of genuine emotions between a man and a woman.

Join us each month for four new titles wherever paperback books are sold.
Enter the world of American Romance.

Amro-1